Oscar Lovell Triggs, James Deans

Tales from the Totems of the Hidery;

Oscar Lovell Triggs, James Deans

Tales from the Totems of the Hidery;

ISBN/EAN: 9783337024208

Printed in Europe, USA, Canada, Australia, Japan

Cover: Foto ©Andreas Hilbeck / pixelio.de

More available books at **www.hansebooks.com**

Tales from the Totems of the Hidery

COLLECTED BY

JAMES DEANS

Edited by Oscar Lovell Triggs

VOLUME II

Archives of the International Folk-Lore
Association

CHICAGO, 1899

EDITORIAL NOTE.

James Deans, the collector of these tales from the Hidery, is widely known as a geologist, ethnologist and anthropologist. He is a Scotchman by nativity, but he has lived for many years on the northwest coast of America., having been sent by the Hudson Bay Company, forty-five years ago, to Fort Victoria on the south end of Vancouver Island, which was the most remote of the trading posts of that company. Mr. Deans has made an intimate study of the natives of the northwest region, and he is probably the only man in the world who is able to translate their tales and interpret their totem marks and crests.

In 1892 Mr. Deans prepared an anthropologic exhibit for the World's Fair, which consisted of one of the ancient native houses and its totem post, found at Skidegat, Queen Charlotte Island, and a reproduction of an entire village of the Haida in model form, with specimens of the utensils, implements, dress, etc., of the people. This exhibit may now be seen at the Field Columbian Museum in Chicago. As a guide to this collection, the present volume will be found of great value. In the appendix is reprinted from the American Antiquarian, a paper of Mr. Deans', describing the totem posts at the Fair.

This publication makes the first authentic collection of Hidery tales in volume form. Mr. Deans has published other accounts of the people and versions of their stories in the American Antiquarian, whose files may be consulted by those interested. But the present volume contains practically all that has been published elsewhere. The references to the Antiquarian are hereby appended : How the Whullemooch Got Fire. Vol. VIII., p. 41 ; How the Mountain Sheep Originated. Vol. VIII., p. 115 ; Yicsack, or the Hat. Vol. VIII., p. 170 ; Haidah Land. Vol. IX., p. 238 ; Inside View of a Haidah Dwelling. Vol. IX., p. 309 ; The Worship of Priapus among the Indians of British Columbia. Vol. IX., p. 368 ; A Strange Way of Preserving peace amongst Neighbors. Vol. X., p. 42 ; The Raven in the Mythology of Northwest America. Vol. X.,(I) p. 109 :

(II)p. 273; The Feast of Ne-Kilst-Lass, the Raven God. Vol X., p. 383 ; The Raven Myth of the Northwest Coast, Resemblance to Certain Bible Stories and Greek Constellations. (III) Vol. XI., p. 297 ; The Haida-kwul-ra, or Native Tobacco of the Queen Charlotte Haidas. Vol. XII., p. 48 ; A Weird Mournful Song of the Haidas. Vol. XIII., p. 52 ; The Story of Skaggy Bealus. Vol. XIII., p. 81 ; Burial Mounds of Vancouver Island and their Relics. Vol. XIII., p. 171 ; Moon Symbol on the Northwest Coast. Vol. XIII., p. 341 ; Carved Columns or Totem Posts of the Haidas. Vol. XIII., p. 282 ; The Antiquities of British Columbia. Vol. XIV., p. 41 ; Totem Posts of the World's Fair. Vol. XV., p. 281 ; A Little Known Civilization. Vol. XVI., p. 208 ; The Hidery Story of Creation. Vol. XVII., p. 61 ; What Patlatches Are. Vol. XVIII., p. 274 ; When Patlatches are Observed. Vol. XVIII., p. 329. Another paper on "Legendary Lore of the Coast Tribes of Northwestern America" was published in Vol. I. of the Archives of the International Folk-Lore Association, p. 266.

A few illustrations are added to the text. The photograph of the group of Indians, in which Mr. Deans also appears, was taken before the Hidery house at the World's Fair. The pictures of the ancient and modern villages are recent photographs, belonging to the collection of the Field Columbian Museum. The figures of the medicine men are native carvings. In one, the doctor is in the act of curing a sick person; a bucket of water stands before the patient, in which the doctor dips his hands after making passes over the sick man. This Skaggy is in full dress. The drawing of the thunder-bird illustrates one of the clan crests. The pipe shows a representation of Wasco. He is bringing whales from the sea; one in his mouth, one across his back, and one held by his tail.

The Association is under great obligations to Mr. Deans, and as ever to Mrs. Bassett, its honored Secretary.

O. L. Triggs.
For the Association.

The University of Chicago.

CONTENTS.

ILLUSTRATIONS.

Tales from the Totems of the Hidery,

And from other Indian Nations on the Coast of North Western America.

INTRODUCTORY.

My object in placing these Folk Tales before the intelligent public, is by doing so there may be chances of preserving them to posterity, because they are rapidly being forgotten, lost beyond a chance of recovery, owing to the passing away of the old folks, whose memories were so well stored with these old tales that they could spend hour after hour and night after night repeating them to admiring listeners seated by the evening lodge fires. In that manner they have been handed down through unknown ages from sire to son. Another means of their preservation was the crest columns, or Totem Poles. As soon as a person had the means, he had to build himself a house, with his totem pole in front of it, with all his crests and all the stories connected with them carved on it. For ages the people were so poor that excepting their own individual crests, none but their chiefs, who alone had the means, were able to have more, and these only on certain conditions, as the following will show. About 1832, a number of whaling ships used to winter, while on the North Pacific, at Skidegat. These whalers came chiefly from Boston or Maine. On one of these ships was a certain Captain Jefferson, who for some reason made up his mind to leave the sea and stay on shore amongst the Hidery. He seems to have had considerable means. On shore he made his home with a family, where he lived a number of years, and died in the latter thirties at the Indian's house, leaving all his money and effects to his host. According to the social laws of the Hidery, when anyone died, leaving his or her property to another, the one who inherited it had also to take the name of the donor. So this family took the name of Jefferson, by which they have been known ever since. Having thus acquired so much additional property, they became the wealthiest family in the village, excepting the chief. This induced him to build a new house with totem pole, showing higher social standing in the tribe. In order to find something to carve on his pole, he adopted a part of the coat of arms of the chief, which he thought he had a right to, his wife being the chief's sister. As soon as the chief knew Jefferson's intentions, he told him that on no account would he allow his crest to be quartered. Jefferson knew it would not do to oppose the chief, so he said : "Skidegat (the chief) won't allow me to take part of his crest, so I will have one of my own made and show him who is richest and at the same time leave no bare space like the poorer people." So when his pole was set up, it had three rows of the tau or copper cross money, one in front and one on each side, in addition to his family crests. When the chief died, Jefferson took down his imitation copper money pole, and in its place put up another with the late chief's coat of arms quartered, including the story connected with it.

As I said before none but chiefs were able to put up elaborately carved columns, with ancient stories on them, up to the years 1830 or later. From that date on to 1880 the Hidery began to go abroad as sailors and otherwise mix with the white settlers, where by labor and other means they acquired money and goods. These were sent home to their relations, in order to help them to have fine houses and totem poles. For that purpose every means was used. Soon the common people became richer than the chiefs and had better houses and more elaborate totem poles. Soon an active competition commenced, each one trying to have the best. Wives, sisters and mothers would prostitute themselves, in order to obtain the wherewith to get ahead of the others. Some died in the mad race for wealth and today the unfinished houses stand a beautiful ruin, sad mementos of the past.

While some were busy with this building and carving, others were busy collecting all the old stories to be found, bearing on their respective crests,. from the old folks and from the ancient mythology of the Hidery. By these means many an old legend and myth, all but forgotten, was revived ; even distant tribes were applied to and many an ancient tale, still lingering in the memories of the old folks, was brought to light. These tales, as soon as found, were carved on the totem poles of the parties, who by the social laws of the Hidery were entitled to them. By these means many an old story was preserved. After a few years of such competition, a change in these people's mode of living took place. All of the old style houses were pulled down and new ones built, with which no totem poles were used; even their old system of crests was broken through, and even these old stories were seldom told. Just then I stept in and collected all I could find, adding greatly to the number I had previously collected. After the lapse of thirty years some of the old stories were so changed that I hardly knew them again. While collecting old Folk Tales the Hidery on the island would borrow from the tribes on the main land and from the tribes beyond the Rocky Mountains. Numbers of these borrowed tales were given a local coloring. Another subject, worthy of notice, is that a large amount of the tales has been taken from the mythology of these people. Others, again, are of great historical value, such as the story of Calcah Jude (Woman of the Ice) and her leadership of the Hidery, when flying before the encroachment of the ice. Also the story of Scannah-gun-nuncus, who fled before the ice coming down the Hunnah, a river on Queen Charlotte Islands. Both of these are of great interest to geologists, even although they are traditions of a long past age. Again the story of Skaggy Bealus is of great value, showing an apparent connection between the Hidery and the rest of the world at a remote period. And yet another, the story of the people, who after the flood, were told by the raven god Ne-kilst-lass to throw stones backward over their heads, which stones on reaching the ground jumped up men and women, seems to be but a version of the Greek myth of Deucalion. These old stories were not borrowed from the white settlers, for the natives knew them ages before the advent of the Yetts Hadray (Iron people), the name given by the Hidery to the white folks, who first gave them iron. While rendering these stories into English, I have kept as near the original as possible. For many years I found great difficulty in getting what I considered a correct version of a story, or a correct reading from the totem poles. This at first was very annoying. and often I felt like giving up my researches; doubtless I would have done so, had it not been that with every succeeding trip to these islands I was able to add a little more to the stock of my information, as well as to clear up many dark points in what I had secured on former visits. Thus gradually was I adding to my knowledge of the social life of the people, as well as an understanding of the carvings on their totem poles. Although I had acquired much, I had still much to learn. In order to get at many things of great importance, I saw plainly that I ought to spend a few months amongst them. During the summer of 1883 I was able to spend a few months somewhat satisfactorily. Starting from Skidegat in a canoe, I visited all the tribes and the most of the villages along the east, north and west coasts of these islands. At these villages, I learned much from the people and from their totem poles. While visiting at the different villages, I found at every one a little variation in their stories, myths and totem poles.

Again in the summer of 1889 I had the opportunity of paying a visit of a few months to the northwest coast, where I also learned much. All my visits to these islands were connected either with geology or coal mines. Of course, I could only give my spare time to my favorite studies. Often I wished I could be able to give them my undivided attention; fortunately, I was able to do so much sooner than I expected. Early in March, 1892, I was sent amongst the Hidery, by the Department of Anthropology of the World's Columbian Exposition, Chicago, with instructions to get a model of a village and of their tombs, and articles of everyday life and use, and also to study their several crests, dances and their Folk Tales. This I gladly did, and before November I had brought together an entire village in miniature, with a large house just as the people lived in it, with also a large quantity of their household goods. All of these I shipped to Chicago without delay. About the middle of March, 1893, George Hunt, of Fort Rupert, Vancouver Island, who had got together a party of Quackutt Indians for the Department of Anthropology, and myself left for Chicago. During the great Fair we built two large houses alongside of the South Pond, one Hidery and one Quackutt; the former was divided into small bed-rooms for our accommodation, and in it we received visitors.

When the Anthropological Building was finished, I put all my miniature houses in place as their originals stood in the land of the Hidery. These strange little houses drew large crowds of visitors each day. While putting them in place I was frequently asked by the visitors to tell what they were. This I gladly did, giving readings from the totem poles, and telling the quaint old stories connected with them. Day after day, from morning to night, I had crowds of admiring listeners, many of whom wished to get a book, or if there were none to be bought, asked me if I could write one telling all about them. This I promised to do, when I got home, if I could find time and the money to do so. For that purpose, a number of ladies and gentlemen gave me their names; each would take one or more copies.

In order that the tales would be better understood, I found it necessary to give a description of the people from whom I gathered these tales, their history, habits and social usages.

I shall first tell of the two phratries, the Raven and Eagle, and afterward give a description of each crest and the stories connected with them.

I have, as far as I know, given a correct account of everything mentioned, and if I have made any mistakes I shall be much pleased to be corrected. As a writer, I cannot and dare not make any pretensions, because I had but little schooling. The extent of it was a little of the three r's, reading, 'riting (writing) and 'rithmetic (Arithmetic.)

With thankful remembrance of the kind friends I met at the World's Fair, to the International Folk Lore Association of Chicago in general, and to its worthy secretary, Mrs. Helen Wheeler Bassett, I submit these stories for consideration.

The Author,
JAMES DEANS,
Victoria, B. C.

Tales from the Totems of the Hidery

And other Indian Nations on the
Coast of North Western America.

Early in the summer of 1852, in my native Scotland, along with several others, I joined the Puget Sound Agricultural Company, a branch of the Hudson Bay Company, as a farm laborer. Toward the end of August, that year, we left London, England, on the Company's barge Norman Morrison, with Captain Wishart, bound for Vancouver Island on the coast of Northwest America, where this Company held large tracts of farming land. After being six months under the care of the good captain, we arrived safely at Royal Roads, outside of Victoria harbor, on Sunday, 16th of January, 1853. On Tuesday, 18th, we all went ashore, at what was then known as Fort Victoria, a trading post of the Hudson Bay Company, now Victoria, the capital of the province of British Columbia. After being on the island a few months I learned enough of the Chinook to enable me to converse as well as to trade with the Indians.

During those early days almost every Indian nation in Northwestern America, now British Columbia, and Sitka, now Alaska, was represented at the fort. These people came south for the purpose of earning goods, such as blankets, printed and white calico, etc., which were sent to their northern homes and which they sold in order to build large houses and raise elaborate totem posts.

As soon as I was able to converse with these people I was surprised to find that each nation had a wonderful mythology, as well as a large amount of Folk Lore. Having made this discovery, my next step was to collect all I could find and write it down, in order to preserve it from oblivion, irrespective of either tribe or nation. During these early days I often heard from the Company's people who had been trading in these northern parts, about the wonderful and mysterious picture writings on the houses of the native people, as well as strange carvings on tall columns, placed in front of every house. They used to tell how the houses appeared as if they had been built in a perfect forest of tall columns. Not only were there paintings on the houses and carvings on their tall columns, but also on the roofs of their houses there were images of bears, ravens and eagles. Often we used to discuss the probable signification of these things, more especially those which resembled buffalos and crocodiles. These discussions were very fruitful of theories as to the motives for their erection and their use. It was an easy matter to discuss as well as to theorize, but it was a harder matter to give a satisfactory explanation of what they were.

In later years, after I had left the Company, I paid a visit to Fort Simpson, one of the northern trading posts. During a stroll through the Indian village, outside of the fort, I was astonished at the amount of carvings and paintings on the houses and tall columns, to be seen everywhere. This visit was made in the summer of 1862, extending up into Alaska, where I also had a chance to look over the carved columns. Early in the spring of 1869 I visited the home of Hidery proper, Queen Charlotte Islands. While there I discovered that every village on these islands was full of paintings and carvings and that there were various sorts of columns, also dead houses, with strange looking animal carvings on them. Seeing so many of these things everywhere, awoke in my mind a determination to study them when I had an opportunity. After this visit ten years passed away before I was able to revisit the islands. During these years, I collected from Indian visitors enough to add considerably to my collection of tales. I was also able to glean a few ideas concerning the carvings from two gentlemen who had made them a study. One was a young man named Samuel Poole, who had lived on these islands a number of years; the other one, Judge Swan of Port Townsend. After a while I was able to spend for several years a few weeks every fall amongst these people. During these visits I was able to learn a deal, which helped greatly to clear up the mystery by enabling me to read the inscriptions on the columns as well as to understand the paintings on the houses and other things.

Although I had learned much, still it was little in so wide a field. Often I wished I could spend a summer in one of their villages in order to study the subject thoroughly. Luckily, I was able to spend one sooner than I expected. In the fall of 1891 I received orders from the Department of Anthropology of the World's Fair, to be held in 1893, at Chicago, to go north as soon as spring opened, in order to secure one of the large Hidery houses just as the people lived in it, also a miniature Hidery village, with its totem poles, mortuary columns, and tombs, also to study their carvings and to collect the Folk Lore, as well as to study the social usages of the Hidery people, their crests, clans and their several dances. I received a sum of money to enable me to buy whatever exhibits I found of any value. Early in the following spring I was under way for Hidery Land. Before I got through in October I had collected and shipped to Chicago the Hidery exhibits, shown at the late great Fair, and now in the Field Columbian Museum in Jackson Park. Besides getting the materials mentioned above I had learned to read the carvings and paintings fairly well.

In order that the readers of these tales may understand something of the people, I shall give a brief discription of them, their country and social usages, beginning with the land they live in.

HIDERY LAND.

The original home of the Hidery was on that group of islands, lying off the north-west coast of North America, named 1787 by Captain Dirion after one of his ships, the Queen Charlotte. These islands lie between 52° and 55° N. L. and between 131° and 135° West Longitude. About 150 years ago, owing to intertribal war, a number of the Hidery living in the northern towns, crossed over to the islands lying off the coast of Southern Alaska. Since that time the Hidery have occupied all the north coast island group and also the Prince of Wales Archipelago. To British Columbia all the Queen Charlotte Island group belong, and to Alaska the other groups. On the west coast the Queen

Charlotte group are mountainous and covered with timber. The eastern parts are level, with large tracts of open land, some of which is swampy, owing to the streams being filled with log jams, which prevents the bottom lands from being drained. The west coast is very wet, while the east is dry. The climate owing to its humidity, is often chilly, but not extremely cold. I have lived on these islands throughout the year and never found the frost below zero. As far as I have seen, all sorts of vegetables may be grown there, fruit trees seem to do well. As for cereals I can only say that wheat, barley and oats have been tried as an experiment and found to ripen, peas do well, so do potatoes, turnips and carrots. Small fruits grow abundantly on the hill sides. Wild strawberries, large and luscious, grow in rich profusion on the new made lands left by a receding sea on a rising land.

There seems to be large quantities of valuable timber on all of these islands, the principal sorts are, first: the western hemlock, Abeis Mertensii and spruce, A. Menzeseii. These sorts are good for lumber and for packing boxes. Of cedars there are two sorts, yellow cedar Cupressus, Neotkatensis, and the large red cedar, Thuja giganteus. Of these, the first is good for fancy work, out of the other the Indians build their houses, make their large canoes and often their dishes. On these islands there are no hard woods, excepting a native crab apple, also a species of alder peculiar to these islands, which is found in great abundance and used as fuel by steamers. The Indians use this wood extensively in their carvings. Naturally this sort of wood gives out a reddish sap which would discolor their carvings. In order to hinder this the Hidery put it through a process which makes it beautiful and white. This is obtained in the following manner: A tree is felled and a piece of it cut to answer the purpose; it is next put into a hot fire where it is kept and turned until thoroughly scorched; then it is laid in the sea, where it soaks, never less than twenty-four hours, when it is taken out and trimmed. When dry it is carved into shape and looks well.

These islands contain extensive fields of coal, bituminous and anthracite. Iron is also found in large quantities. Gold, silver, copper and lead have also been found in various places.

There is a soft black slate, found on one of the islands, out of which the people make large numbers of their carvings. In several places are salt springs, some forming quite large streams. Fisheries are extensive along the coasts, such as salmon, herrings, halibut, sturgeon and cod. Of cod, there are three sorts, viz. : red, black and true cod. The rivers also abound with trout. These rivers, although numerous, are generally small, rapid and shallow; some are clear, others are as black as rum. On the higher mountains, snow lingers all the year. Of wild animals, there are sea and land otters, martins and black bears. Such is Hidery Land.

THE HIDERY PEOPLE—THEIR NAME.

The most of writers spell their name Haida, Hydah. Their name, as pronounced by themselves, is Hidery, which signifies people, when they, themselves, are meant. All other people are pronounced Hawdry.

In personal appearance, they are taller and fairer than their cousins on the mainland, many resembling Chinese, while others are Japanese in feature. Tradition says the darker people came from Alaska, and the fairer ones are the descendants of three Chinamen who were cast ashore on the southern end of these islands ages ago, who married and lived with the tribes. They are a very ingenious people, excelling in carving; not only do they excell in wood carving, as was shown in their exhibit at the late great Chicago Fair, and which is still to be seen in the Field Columbian Museum in Jackson Park, in that city, but also in the black slate of their country. They are also proficient workers in gold and silver. They all make good sailors and often ship to distant ports. Socially they are divided into four classes, namely: chiefs, nobles, common people and Skaggy or medicine men. The chieftancy is hereditary. Failing heirs, either one nearest of kin to the chief, or one of influence in the village takes the office, or if the chief leaves a widow, she, if she wishes, takes her late husband's place. The office of chief is to preside at the council of a tribe, to settle disputes or lead on the braves in times of war, to give names and confer titles and honors on members of his tribe, male or female. The chief is to a certain extent supported by his tribe, as I will show by and by. The nobles and common people differ but little, though to a certain extent distinct, because any boy or girl by being saving and industrious may one day become the highest in their land. As soon as one acquires property, or enough to pay for it, the chief gives him a good and honorable name, he at first having been given an ugly, nasty one, one he was ashamed of, in order to make him try for a better one. Every time he is able to invite others of his own tribe, as well as neighboring ones, to a great "give-away," he gets a higher name as well as rank. Money with them as well as with many others, is an "open sesame" and leads to higher crests and more black and white bands on their mortuary columns. Their rank is shown by red, white and black bars. Thus the bears have their *tan gue, or bear's ears, the beavers have their marks on the tail. Rank is also shown by the tattoo marks, which the young men have on their breasts and the young women on their arms and legs. Amongst these people, the bigger the labret or lip piece, the higher the rank among the women folks. Medicine men and women, or medicine folks, are named skaggy, that is an abbreviation of skah gillda or long haired ones ; so named, because, both sexes wore their hair long and tied up in a crown knot. In by-gone days the skaggy held the office of priest as well as doctor. As a priest, being clairvoyant, he was generally consulted on the affairs of this life as well as the next. This will be shown in the tales. A skaggy's outfit consisted of a medicine rattle, a rod or staff of office, a couple of sharp pointed bones, one of which he usually held in his hand, the other in a hole made for it through the division of the nostrils. He also wore a necklace of sharks' teeth. Around his waist he wore an apron fringed with puffins' beaks, named by the Hidery coohan. The female skaggy had a couple of circles strung with beaks. These she held, one in each hand, which with her every movement would make a rustling sound. These were the clecha darran. Of these things, the rattle was used to scare away the trouble, as well as to give notice of the arrival of the skaggy. The pointed bones were used to probe any abscess or such like. The staff was about four feet long, carved all over with mystic symbols. When the medicine man

---

*Tan, a black bear—gue, ears.

arrived at any sick person's bed he would knock on the floor,
then poke the sick party, saying: "get up, get up." If able the
patient did so, if not other means were tried. The skaggy always
reminded me of the priests as represented on the tablets of palen-
que, and others of the ruined cities of South America. When
the skaggy died he was always wrapt in mats and blankets and
his body laid away in a house prepared as his tomb, or sathling-
un nah, on some lonely rock or island, with two or more wooden
images outside as guardians of the body. These were known
amongst the Hidery by the names of cull-stum-gay and ligga
deich, the latter name being borrowed from the Simsheans.
These sort of beings are represented as male and female, having
the body of a man or woman with legs like a goat, a sort of
satyr, who lived in woodlands and among the mountains. They
are represented as being great thieves from whom nothing could
be hidden, so in order to prevent the real cull-stum-gays from
stealing the body, the skaggy's relations had dummies placed
outside.

THE HIDERY AS GAMBLERS.

The Hidery, like the Chinese to-day, used to be inveterate
gamblers. They had three modes of gambling, first, by having
a small bit of wood concealed in the hand while the opposite
party guessed which hand it was in; the second was by moving
a number of wooden discs under the hand while covered
with fine cedar bark fibre; the third style was by a number of painted sticks about three inches in length, in pairs—how
they played with them I can hardly tell. Several years ago they
left off all sort of chance games. They used to be so fond of
gambling that I have known them to lose all they had, leaving
themselves stark naked.

HIDERY HOUSES.

In building their houses the Hidery followed one general
plan, with modifications according to rank or social standing.
For instance, some had totem posts in front and inside of their
houses, while others were only painted showing the crest of its
owners. The second house in the model Hidery village at the
late World's Fair at Chicago, the house on the left of the stream,
belonged to this sort. It is one of the moon crest, as is shown by

THE SITE OF AN ANCIENT VILLAGE.

the painted moon on the front of the house. Of this I shall treat more fully while speaking of the moon clan and its tales. The third painted house in the above collection, was another of this style of house, but connected with the bear clan. The painting on the front was a bear's face, whence its name of *chooity a chlechia*, that is, bear's mouth. This house was the meeting place of the bear clan. Of this I shall say more while speaking of the bear clan.

HIDERY HOUSES—HOW BUILT.

In length, the houses of these people ranged from thirty to sixty feet, or even more; in width, from twenty-nine to fifty feet. Some houses had an excavation from the surface to a depth of from six to ten feet. To the chiefs only belonged this kind of house. The common people could not afford to make them. The sides of this hole were cribbed with heavy cedar beams, ten feet inside from the walls. This space was divided into compartments, having an upper floor with hatches. In these divisions, everything easily hurt by frost was kept. All the floors of their houses, excepting a piece five feet square for a fire-place, were covered with heavy planking. This fire-place was filled with clean sea gravel. When dirty, it was cleaned out and refilled, the refuse being cast on shore, forming a midden. In the roof, above the fire-place, was the smoke-hole. Every house had four heavy corner posts deeply sunk in the ground. Each of these posts had a mortice through which heavy cross beams were placed, in order to form the roof. On these boards were placed long cedar beams, six in number, three being on each side. The two lowest of the six were grooved throughout their whole length, the groove being placed downward. On the surface of the ground were also placed six broad beams, also grooved, these grooves being placed upward. In order to form the walls, broad cedar boards were forced along into these grooves. Two sorts of covering were used for the roof by the Hidery, cedar bark and cedar boards. Sometimes boards only were used and sometimes both, the boards beneath and the bark on top. Inside of the houses were little rooms, big enough for a bed and chair, with sometimes a small table. These small bed-rooms were portable and would be moved to any part of the house according to fancy.

None of the houses had upper floors, instead a large number of poles was suspended from the roof, for drying fish and hanging fishing tackle, etc.

All sorts of food were served on the floor in wooden dishes. Flesh meats were held in dishes, and after being cut into small pieces by bone or copper knives, were passed to the mouth by the fingers. They used spoons for all sorts of soups; these spoons were made from deer horns as well as carved out of wood; the spoon handles were nicely ornamented by squares of abalone shells, glued fast into the handles by glue made from halibut fins boiled down.

Every town was named after its chief, such as Skidegat's town, after its chief Skidegat; Gumshewa's town after its chief Gumshewa. Besides these they had other names, such as Illth-cah-getla, the Hidery name for Skidegat. Every house had a characteristic name, as *nah clechas*, new house; *nah yonans*, large house; *noo gah deelans*, thunder and lightning house— so named by the man who built it, meaning he had the best house; *coot-cuh-towel-cah-coot-coo-nah*, rain-bow house, or pathway of the angels house. According to Hidery belief, when the end of a rainbow seemingly rested on the roof of a house, it was said to be the pathway of the angels, bringing blessings to the people living in this house. *Sen-i-coot-quin-nie*, was the house of contentment, or contented people's house, and *nah-qweega-heegin*, wind-sounding house. Often a house had on its roof something to show its name. For instance, a house in the village of Skidegat had a raven on top of each front corner post, showing its name to be raven house, *choo-e-ah nass*. This house stood on the south end of the model village at the great Chicago Fair.

When the people living in a house had lots of boxes, or one for a door step, they got the name of *cotta-nass-hidery*, box-house people. If the people living in a house had lots of copper cross T money, they got the name of *tau-scho-ass hidery*, or copper tau (T) house people. Many years ago while building a house on the south end of Queen Charlotte Islands, there happened a severe earthquake, clagah heeldans. So ever after this house was known as *nah rah heeldans*, house of the shaking. Often while building a stylish house, the owner would have

an image of a man on top of the two front corner posts, a representation of himself, for instance. Many years ago a rich Hidery,
named *Ellzu-wuss*, was building himself a second house, on which
as above, was placed an image of himself. Looking over it when
finished, he was so pleased with it that he exclaimed, '' I have
the best house in town, a regular thunder and lightning one.'' So
there and then it was named *noo-gah-deelans*—thunder and lightning house. The two images had on long hats or taden skeels, representing high social standing. In the miniature village in Chicago
is a house which has on the ends of its six roof-beams six heads
all hanging down; in the original house at Skidegat, each head
had hair fixed on it, which waved in the wind. On that account
it got the name of six heads house, *cadzo-clou-oonal-nass*. The owner
of this house and his fore-bears have taken that name but shortened
to *clads-ah-coon*. The family bearing this name was *ellzu cath-
lans-coon-hidery*, or chief of the point of the waves people. Several generations ago these people chose a beautiful point of land,
whereon to build their village, on the east of Queen Charlotte
Island, known by the above name Point of the Waves. Some
time after they got settled an immense tidal wave carried off the
entire village. Five times it was destroyed and four times re-
built. Unable to rebuild any longer, the chief, by the request of
his people, went and bought a piece of land from the people of
Skidegat, lying at the east end of the village. To this they all
removed with their belongings and here they made a home for
themselves, led by the old chief. In their new home all the
houses were arranged as they stood in the old one; following the
same order their descendants live to-day still retaining their old
tribal name, point of the waves people, even the new style houses
keeping the old names.

Although these old-time houses long ago gave place to newer
styles, yet by help from the old folks I was able to represent, in
miniature, for the Fair, this old village.

Now, with regard to the six heads mentioned above, the following will explain. While this chief and his people were building on the point he was unable to settle on the plan of his new
house. While in this dilemma, he one night dreamed of or saw
in a vision, a plan of a complete house with totem post and all,

with this difference; he saw on the ends of the six roof-beams
the same number of human heads placed upside down, their long
hair waving in the wind.   He was told in the dream to go and
build his new house like it.   This he did and ever after, both at
the Point of the Waves and later at Skidegat his descendants
have used the six heads for the same purpose, until a few years
ago, when the house was pulled down, in order to be reproduced
after the white people's style.   The model of this house, which
I got for the great Fair, was made by a descendant of the chief
who first made the six heads.   Images were put on houses for
various purposes.   The one I am about to speak of was made out
of revenge for a supposed insult, as the following will show.   On
the tops of the two front corner posts, in a house belonging to
one of the better class, whose name was Gsthlans, in the above
mentioned village of Skidegat, a number of years ago, were
two images, which could easily be recognized as other than
Hidery.   On the left of the observer, was one with a long hat
and frock coat.   The other, on the right, had on a cap with a
peak in front.   The first represented the police magistrate of this
city, Victoria; the other represented George Smith Clark of the
above city.   In or about the summer of 1870, this Gathlans left
Skidegat, in order to have a few months sojourn in Victoria, seeing the, to him, strange houses and improvements of the new
comers.   While in Victoria, one day he got jolly drunk and in
good fighting trim; the noise he made was such that it soon
brought along the police, who quickly had him locked up.   Next
day, feeling sadly out of repair, he was up before the above mentioned magistrate, Judge Pemberton, charged with being drunk
and disorderly.   After conviction, he was fined $50, or six
months imprisonment.   Not having the money to pay his fine,
he was locked up; after a few days, his friends, who had raised
the money, came and paid his fine, which gave him his liberty.
For the loss of so much money and the insult to his dignity, by
being in prison, he was determined to have his revenge, and this
is how he thought he had it.   Smarting under his supposed insult, he took the earliest opportunity to get home, where he lost
no time in setting a carver to make a couple of effigies of the
judge and his clerk, which, when finished, were placed on his

house-top, in hopes that every passer-by would jeer and mock the originals through their representations. By doing so he fancied he had his revenge. A few years afterwards I visited the village, and while there I saw the images and heard their story. When I returned to Victoria, I gave a short account of it in one of the local newspapers. Some time after I met the Judge, who inquired if the story was true ; when I told him it was, he thought it a capital joke, and told me he had fined several of the Hidery for the same offense, in a like sum.

While amongst these people in the summer of 1892, I was surprised to see how changed the place was: all the houses built in the olden times, with the exception of three, had been pulled down, in order to make room for the march of civilization. Seeing the change, I made inquiry as to the whereabouts of the two effigies, wishing to take them home with me. I was told, that after they were taken down they stood in a wood shed a long time, and finally were cut up for fire wood.

PATLATCHES.

Patlatches, or give away. This is the Chinook name of the great feast or give away. Each nation on this western slope used to reckon on having one at least every year. Patlatches was a custom or mode of sending out invitations, paying debts, as well as acquiring new names, honors, etc., by giving a great feast and making presents to all the invited guests. For instance, when a chief of a tribe had acquired property and wished to rank higher in the social forms of his tribe and nation, a number of his tribemen would be sent in all directions, wherever there was a village, in order to invite all who wished to come, to be at his village on a certain day. The invited ones very seldom failed to make their appearance ; some came to pay their debts and again get into debt deeper than before. Those from a certain village or district generally came in a body of from five to twenty or more canoes, as the case might be. If there happened to be any big guns in the village, the visitors were welcomed by a salute. As the visitors drew near, all the people in the village came out and squatted in front of their houses, or sat in groups within hearing of the visitors, who at the same time rested on their oars, keeping afloat a few yards from the shore. Meanwhile, both parties would sit from ten to fifteen minutes without exchanging a word. Then a movement is seen in one of the canoes to get together a few bundles of split cedar, each piece about fourteen inches in length and as thick as a man's finger, and to place them alongside of the chief. When these bunches were untied, the chief arose and harangued the people on shore, throwing at the same time these splints one by one ashore. As soon as one was thrown, another was passed up to the speaker, who kept on talking and throwing until all had been thrown ashore. The sticks represented goods obtained at a former patlatch, which were returned with interest, and they also represented presents which the visitors were making, presents for which they expected to be repaid double, according to aboriginal usage. The chief, in his harangue, said : "We have come from such and such a place by your invitation. These sticks represent the amount of goods received from you while here before; we return the same amount with interest, two for one; also we bring you presents, which doubtless you will accept." When done with talking, he would sit down. Then the village chief would say a few words by way of welcome ; meanwhile all the canoes were making for shore, to which they quickly passed all their belongings. Seeing this, all the people in the village hastened down to help them. Very soon everything was snugly stowed away and the canoes hauled safely above high water. While all this was being enacted, a meal was being prepared by the villagers who gave the feast. When ready, all had to come and partake. In olden times their food consisted chiefly of deer, bear and seal meat, with often tidbits from whales added; along with these were wild fowls, roots and berries. The flesh meats were generally cut up into small pieces, according to circumstances, neither knives nor forks, only spoons, being used. The food, when ready, was emptied into troughs of various lengths, cut out of a block of wood ; these were placed in rows along the floor; along both sides of them the people squatted and picked up the pieces with their fingers, while for the soup the spoon was used. Quite a change has come over these feasts of late years by the use of tea, coffee, bread and butter, also preserves and many other things. After the feast, the remainder of the day was spent singing and dancing. Before the give away commences, the chief, or whosoever gives it, gets all his goods in order, blankets, canoes, paints, and such like, and money, if any. If he thinks there is not enough to meet the demand, he borrows from other members of the tribe. When the time for giving away arrives, the chief mounts on the roof of his house, or on a platform raised for that purpose, with a pile of goods before him, while all the people are gathered below. Then he commences by throwing a blanket to one, a shirt to another, telling a certain one in the crowd to take a canoe in a certain place, and so forth, until all have been given away. Often a scramble took place. Three or four would catch hold of a blanket and none of them would let go until it was torn to shreds. Then one would give the others so much for their pieces, sew them together and use them. When money was given away, it was either given to certain parties, or scattered amongst the crowd; sometimes it was thrown into shallow water. Then came fun for the naked boys and girls. The chief, who gave the patlatch, although he got himself a better name as well as higher social standing by doing so, was always left in poverty, but not long, because as I said before, everything given away had to be returned, often double ; that is to say, for every single article given away, two had to be returned. Sometimes, when people of different nations and languages were invited, then all of the tribe were expected to help without returns. At these patlatches, the higher the standing in the social scale of the man or woman, the more he got. When anyone built a new house, a patlatch was given to all who helped, as well as to invited friends.

The most important part of a house was the gayring or carved column, totem post, as it is generally named. In order to have one, the first act was for a party to go into the woods and select a tree of a given size, as near as possible to the sea. When a suitable one was found, it was cut down and hewn to certain dimensions; then it was slid into the water, where a party was in waiting in a canoe, who hauled it to the village and put it on shore. On shore, it went into the hands of the carvers, who hewed it into shape, then marked one side of it into sections. The average height of these columns was thirty feet, divided into five sections of six feet each.   For carving each of these sections ten blankets were paid, or, in all, fifty blankets.   These blankets were bought by the bale for not less than five dollars per blanket, which would make two hundred and fifty dollars for each post. Generally the party who carved one section, say the lower, was not allowed to carve the next, unless his social standing allowed him to do so, and in like manner, through all the five sections different carvers were employed.   When finished, all the villagers helped to raise it.   If they were unable to do so, help was secured from another village.   If a man happened to die while his house was in course of erection, nothing more was done to it.   At Skidegat I saw a column lying rotting, which had been ready for the carver when the owner died.   The carvings always showed the social standing of the heads of the family ; the wife's on top of the column, because she ranked highest in the family circle ; that of the husband occupied its lower half.   The social standing of the Hidery was represented in three divisions or crests.   First, the sexual crest ; second, the clan; and third, the secret society crest. Apart from these three was the totem.   The sexual crest was inherited from the mother and passed through her from her grandmother to all of her children ; for example, if the mothers were "bears," all the children were the same, boys and girls.   The girls, in turn, when they became mothers, gave their bear crest to the children, the father's crest going for nothing.   The clan, or family crest was held by every member of the family.   The society crest could only be got and held by initiation into the order, and often cost large sums to obtain.   The totems were any animals, birds, or any thing living, which crossed a child's path when first trying to move about ; or, any thing a child tried to say, such as deer, dog or bear, etc.   This became his or her totem ; that is, guardian angel, through life.   Totems, as far as I have been able to learn, have long been in disuse among the Hidery.

Hidery crests were divided into two great phratries, or brotherhoods, represented by the raven, named by the Hidery, Choo-e-ah, and the eagle, named choot.   These two large phratries were represented by a number of smaller crests; for example, the raven had eleven crests, namely : wolf, bear, scannah or killer whale, skate, mountain goat, sea-lion, chee-moose or snag-in-a-river,

moon, sun, rainbow and scamsum or thunder bird. The eagle
has the following, fourteen in all : eagle, raven, frog, beaver,
shark, moon, duck, codfish, wasco, whale, owl, dogfish, sculpin,
and dragon fly. Each of these crests had their respective
dances, as well as musical instruments, by which they imitated
the call of their individual crests. Their dances also were in
imitation of the walk of the subject adopted. Connected with
these crests and dances were circles of cedar bark of various colors.
These circles represented various degrees. For instance, one circle
denotes one degree, while two circles denote two degrees, and so
onward.

Before I take up the tales, there are a few things of importance. On top of a number of columns is an image with a
tall hat marked off into three or four divisions; on others,
are two or three images with hats. The single one with the taden
skeel, or long hat, is a chief or a person of two or three degrees
standing, as is shown by his hat. When there are three images
with taden skeel, this, in some instances, shows that the chief
who built this house was succeeded by one or two brothers, as
the case might be. According to the Hidery legends, these three
images were adopted by an old chief, Skidegat, from a very old
story, which runs thus : Long ago, Ne-kilst-lass, the raven god,
turned himself into a beautiful woman and three men fell in love
with her. The three men have been used by the descendants of
the old chief who adopted them. Again, it was customary in
old times, when a man was building a house, to kill a slave and
put his body into the hole made for the gayring, which, when
raised, was placed on the body. In order to show that a slave
had been killed, an image of a man with his head down was
carved on the gayring. The Hidery say they never killed a slave
for that purpose, but instead they sold a slave for what he or she
was worth, and at the same time had a man carved with his head
down. The Hidery told me that their plan for collecting their
just debts when due, was to ask for payment three times, and if still
unpaid after that, the debtor was never again dunned. Although
he was not again asked for payment, other means were employed
for its recovery, as follows : Seeing that nothing could be done by
dunning, the creditor had a gayring erected in front of his house,

on which was carved an image of the debtor with his head down, while on the column beside the image, in order the better to show who the debtor was, one or all of his crests were carved. The Hidery tell me that this scheme never failed; often, when the debtor saw what was being done, he came and paid all in order to save himself from the disgrace. All of the Indians are very proud and quickly resent an insult. If the one who gives the offense wishes to hear no more of it, by way of an apology, he pays a certain number of blankets. If the one who gives the offense objects to doing so, the other destroys a certain amount of his property before the villagers. As soon as the offender sees what is being done, he, too, destroys the same amount and ends the trouble. If the offender destroys more than the other, he is declared to be the better man. If the offender objects to the destruction of his property, he is despised by all the villagers. If he is a poor man and has nothing to destroy, then he, too, is despised for being poor. If one man, when building a house, took part of a crest belonging to another, thinking he had a right to it, the man from whom it was taken called together a council of the tribe, at which the rights of both parties were discussed. If the decision was against the thief, he was expected to give up all claim to the parts which he took. If he refused to do so, the next thing in order was the destruction of property. Whoever destroyed the most kept the crest. I have heard of a case in which both of the contestants were left in poverty.

RELIGIOUS BELIEF OF THE HIDERY.

Until lately these people believed in a Supreme Being, whose name was Ne-kilst-lass. Under that name, he was the creator and preserver of every thing. Under other names, he was the cause or originator of every discordant and evil action or principle. In all of his works of creation and providence, he assumed the form of a raven, by which name he was understood by every nation in Northwestern America. In Alaska he was known by the name of Yethel or Yale; amongst the Hidery he was known by the name of Choo-e-ah. The Hidery believe that God, that is, Ne-kilst-lass, is the common father of all and that all mankind was developed from his connection with a cockle, and the evolution of the race was the natural outcome of every succeeding gen-

A VILLAGE WITH MODERN HOUSES.

eration, the fittest as well as the best looking being chosen. They believe that every one possesses an undying soul, and in eternal progression after death. The body, they say, is never resurrected. Until lately they held communion with the spirits of their departed relations. With them the female is the ruling principle in nature. This was shown in almost everything connected with the social life of the Hidery. The wife was the head of the house. She gave her name and her crest to her children. The phallic idea was a marked feature in their belief. The entrance to their houses was by an oval hole cut through the main carved column or gayring. This was a symbolization of the female generative organ. Every time a person came out of or went into the house he was reminded of his advent into the world. So strong, at one time, was the phallic belief amongst them, that their women, after puberty, considered it their duty to encourage at all times sexual intercourse.

THE HIDERY TO-DAY.

In general, the Hidery are great on money making. They would do almost any thing in that line, and for everything they expect a return. "Give nothing for nothing," is their motto. These people have changed astonishingly during the past ten years. As fast as they could get lumber, they pulled down the old houses and built new ones after our style. . All their old dresses, dancing and otherwise, were sold as fast as they could find a buyer. Unfortunately, they cut down for fire wood their beautifully carved totem poles and made no more, except small ones carved out of the black slate of those islands. When I was amongst them lately, I never saw any drunkenness; besides they had become honest. The greatest ambition of the Hidery to-day is to have a fine marble tombstone to mark his or her grave. Generally they have the crest to which they belonged placed on top. On these stones were carved the name and supposed age of the party at death. Often a party saved enough money and bought his own tombstone, having the place and date of his birth engraved on it, with a space left to fill up after death, fearing his relations would keep the money and not buy him a stone as he wished. I once got a sum of money from a Hidery named Jeremiah Smith, in order to get him a marble tombstone, with his crest, an eagle, I think, and the following inscription carved on it :

Erected to the memory of old Jeremiah Smith.
Born at Chah-atill, Queen Charlotte Islands,
Some time in 1823,
And departed this life at Heeni Maud Island,
Queen Charlotte Islands,
On the ——, in the year ——, aged ——.

After I had it made and sent to his home, he stowed it away, saying, "Now I am content, because I know I have a stone." He lived a number of years after that and when he died his relatives had the stone set up on his grave. Whether the blank was ever filled or not, I never heard. After this brief description, the reader will have some idea of the Hidery and their antecedents. There yet remains a great deal of interesting matter untold.

I shall now give the crests and along with them their stories. While doing so, a deal of interesting matter omitted in order to avoid repetition, will be given. I shall begin with the two phratries : first, the raven ; then, the eagle. While giving the crests, I shall show their connection with the Hidery, in particular.

TALES FROM THE RAVEN CREST.

As I have already said, there are amongst the Hidery two great phratries or brotherhoods, the raven and the eagle, so named, because one brotherhood is represented by the raven and the other by the eagle. Amongst the Hidery the raven has eleven gens or crests in its phratry ; the eagle has fourteen. In some villages the raven ranks highest ; in others, the eagle. As a phratry and as a crest, both have their songs and dances, as well as their musical instruments and stories. These instruments were used only to give the call or cry of the bird or animal which represented the coat of arms of the family, or clan. Besides being used as a totem, the raven had higher dignity than all the others, inasmuch as he was a symbolization of the god Ne-kilst-lass, who in all his works of creation and providence assumed the form and features of a raven, whence the habit of all the aborigines of these northern lands using the name of the raven while speaking of their ancient deity. Under the name of Ne-kilst-lass, he was the originator and perfecter of all good. By other names he was known as the originator of all evil. He had no beginning, neither will he have an end. In the shape of a raven before this world existed, he brooded over the intense darkness, until after eons of ages, by the constant flapping of his wings, he beat down the darkness into solid earth. After the earth became solid, the light on its surface was dim and misty, so in order to light up the new formed globe, according to the Hidery, Ne-kilst-lass traveled far and wide for that purpose. During his travels he heard of a chief who lived far away, who had the sun, moon and stars in three separate boxes; so to this chief he went to try what could be done with him. When the chief was asked for the boxes he refused to let him have even one. While Ne-kilst-lass was there, he noticed that the chief had a good looking daughter ; so he went away and turned himself into a nice looking boy and wandered back to the chief's house. When the chief saw him he told him to come in and stay awhile. This the boy gladly did. After awhile the boy and girl took a great fancy to each other. After a while the girl coaxed her father to let the boy have one of those boxes, so he gave him the one which held the stars. Then a little while after, in the same manner he got the second box which held the moon. Afterward he begged hard for the box which held the sun. This, the chief at first refused to part with, but after repeated requests from the young folks, he at last let it go. As soon as the god possessed all the boxes, he placed them on high where they have been ever since, giving light to the world.

ANOTHER VERSION.

The Cowitchians of Vancouver Island say that Queenia, a sort of duck which swims about in flocks and whose cry is called by the white people "sou sou southerly," had the three boxes containing the heavenly bodies. These he always took with him in his canoe when he went fishing, for the double purpose of having light to fish and being afraid lest they should be stolen. Spaul, the raven god, being anxious to get hold of them, asked Queenia to part with them, in order to place them in the heavens and give light to the world. This Queenia refused to do, so Spaul said no more about them. After he and Queenia had been out fishing together a few days, he again asked for them; to his request Queenia gave a refusal. Hearing this, Spaul pitched him overboard and held him down until drowned; he then returned ashore, leaving poor Queenia behind in the water. As soon as Spaul got on dry land he opened the boxes and set up the lights on high, where they have remained ever since, giving light to the world.

ANOTHER VERSION.

The tribes on the rivers Naas and Skeena have another version of this story. They say that, long ago, an old chief lived, with his only daughter, where the Naas now flows, who had all the light in three boxes. These Cauch, the raven god, wanted to get in the worst way, and for a time tried to get hold of them without success. At length he hit on a plan. He noticed that the daughter went to the well every day for a supply of water. While there she often had a drink. So he turned himself into the needle-like leaf of the spruce tree and floated on her drinking water and was swallowed by her. In due season she gave birth to a son who was none other than Ne-kilst-lass, or Cauch, who by this means was born into the family. He quickly grew up to be a big boy and became a great favorite with his grandfather, who spoiled him by letting him have all he asked for. One day he asked the old man for one of the boxes, in order, he said, to play with it. This the old man sturdily refused to grant. Being determined to have all of them, sooner or later, he raised such a row in the family as only a spoiled youngster could, that the old man had no peace, till at length he got angry and pointing to a box he said, "Here, take that one and play with it until you get tired." So he quickly took the box and rolled it about until he got it outside, when he took it up and dashed it to pieces, letting out a flood of light, because it was the sun box he had got. So he took the sun and placed it on high, where it has been giving light to the world ever since. Having got the sun box his next step was to get the other two. Knowing well he could not play the old game he thought of another. Having heard that the old chief had gone up the river fishing for oulachans, he made for himself a false moon, and took a canoe and went up the river to meet Settin-ki-jess, the old chief's name. While the chief was fishing he usually took the moon out of its box in order to give him light, because he always fished after dark. Before getting near to the chief's house the raven god hid the false moon under his coat of feathers. When he reached the place where the chief dwelt it was quite dark. The chief said to the raven, "How do you see to get about in the dark when you have no moon?" "Oh, well enough," replied the raven, "I have a moon of my own," at the same time raising up his feathers and letting out a little light. When Settin-ki-jess saw that his moon was not as he believed it to be, the only one in the world, he lost all conceit of it and the stars and left the two boxes lying about. His neglect was the raven's opportunity who opened the two boxes and let out their contents, which were placed in the heavens, where they have been ever since and will be to the end.

ANOTHER HIDERY VERSION.

Engraven on one or two of the totem poles attached to the little houses in the miniature village I sent to the Chicago World's Fair, was a raven shown in the act of flying up with something in his beak, painted blue and as big as a dollar. This represents a version of the Hidery story of how Choo-e-ah, the raven god, got the sun. According to the story, he heard that a great chief living in a distant part of the country had the sun in a box, so in order to get it he went to the chief's house and after a while found where the precious sun was kept. He said nothing to any one about his plans, so when all were asleep he opened the box and taking the sun in his beak was about to fly out of the smoke-hole in the roof (the name in Hidery parlance is kinet), when he noticed it was closed. So he called to some one on the roof, "Ah, kinet; ah, kinet; open kinet, open kinet." So they opened the smoke-hole and he flew away with the sun and placed it on high.

HOW THE RAVEN GOT FRESH WATER.

At first and long after, all the water on the earth was salt, so Yethel, the Alaskan raven god, (this is a tale of Alaska) being anxious to have streams of fresh water, and on looking over the world for a supply, heard that Canook (wolf), who lived on an island, had all that sort of water in the world in his house. So, in order to get a supply, he took his canoe and sailed over. On the way he met Canook going home from where he had been fishing. Together they gladly went along until they reached the island. Yethel, by invitation from Canook, went to pass the night in his house. This was all he wanted, because he could the better get at the water. In order to prevent any one from stealing the water, Canook used to sleep over his well. Before going to bed he used to draw a bucket full for family use. After supper they all went to bed, where they lay and chatted until Canook fell asleep. After a while, when Yethel thought every one was asleep, he got up and drank all the water. Just as he had finished, some of the family awoke and seeing the empty bucket, called to Canook that Yethel had drunk all the water. Hearing this and fearing Canook, Yethel quickly flew up to the smoke-hole in order to make his escape. Having drunk so much water, he had swelled so large that he stuck fast in the smoke-hole and could not get out either way. Canook, having got up and seeing the state of affairs, piled green wood on the fire, which made a dense smoke that changed Yethel from being a pure white bird to one of a coal black hue. As soon as Yethel got out he flew over to the main land, letting fall a few drops of water as he passed along. Wherever these drops fell, they quickly sprang up rivers, so by means such as these all our rivers on this coast had their origin. Having made the rivers, his next step was to stock them with fish, particularly salmon and oulachan.

ORIGIN OF FISH, HIDERY VERSION.

When Choo-e-ah, the raven god, was looking for salmon to put in the newly formed rivers, he was informed Tsing (beaver) had all the salmon, so in order to get a quantity he turned himself into a beautiful boy and went to the beaver's house. When old Tsing saw a nice looking boy outside, he told him to come inside and live with him awhile. This the boy gladly did. Very soon he gained the old beaver's favor by making himself generally useful. Whenever Tsing went fishing he left the boy at home, and would neither tell him about his salmon nor where he got them. One day, after a meal of salmon, the boy asked him where he got such nice fish. Tsing told him that he had a lake and a river full of them. Hearing this, the boy asked him for a few, if he could spare them, in order, he said, to place them in the rivers and lakes on earth. "No," replied the beaver, "they are exclusively my property and I cannot part with any of them." Seeing the state of affairs, the boy said no more, but awaited his own time. After this the boy was more than ever attentive to the wants and wishes of the old chief, who after a while took him to help while fishing. Gradually, more and more, the beaver got less suspicious of the boy and finally would stay at home and send him. For a long time the boy would return at evening, bringing a supply of better fish than even the beaver himself could bring. All the while the boy was collecting a goodly supply for future use. So one day, when all was ready, he took the fish he had selected and left for the new made rivers, in which he placed male and female salmon. These, in time, filled the lakes and rivers and afterward afforded a supply of salmon for mankind. This is how Ne-kilst-lass put the salmon in the rivers, lakes and streams. Having secured a supply of salmon, his next step was to obtain a supply of oulachans, with which to fill certain rivers.

HOW CAUCH, THE RAVEN GOD, GOT OULACHANS.

This is a tale of the Simshians. Cauch knew that Settin-ki-jess had all this sort of nice little fish and knew that on no account would he part with them. So, in order to get them, he made a canoe out of an old rotten log and started off to overhaul the chief. One thing he wanted to get was oulachan scales with which to besmear his canoe. As Cauch was going along he saw a shag. He knew that that bird, as a companion of this Settin-ki-jess, had access to his store of oulachans, and consequently would have his stomach full. In order to get the shag to await them he contrived that the seagull and the shag should quarrel by telling each that the other had spoken evil of him. At last he got them together, when, after an angry conversation, they followed his advice and began to fight. After a while he urged them to fight harder and to lay on their backs and to kick out with their feet. This they did, and finally the shag threw up the oulachans, which the raven god immediately seized. Having got them he rubbed himself and his old canoe with the oulachan scales, the better to deceive the chief; then coming by night to the old chief's lodge, said that he was very cold and wished to warm himself, as he had been making a great fishery of oulachans, which he had left somewhere not far off. Settin-ki-jess said that could not be true as he alone possessed that sort of fish. Then Cauch Ne-kilst-lass invited him to look at his clothes and at his canoe. Finding both covered with scales, he became convinced that there were in existence other oulachans than his, so in disgust he turned all his stock loose, saying, at the same time, that every moon they would run up certain streams and so continue forever.

THE ORIGIN OF MANKIND.

When Ne-kilst-lass had the world fitted up as a fit abode for a race of beings, one day as he was walking along Nai-coon (long nose) long and sandy beach, he found a cockle, with which he had sexual connection. At the end of nine months he again passed that way. When he came to the cockle he heard sounds coming from it somewhat resembling peep-peep. This was the cockle in labor, which gave birth to six children, of whom the god was father. These six partook of both sexes. From three he took away the female principle, while from the other three he took away the male, making them male and female, three of each. In the abdomen of the three females he placed a sea snail. Having done so he told them that by two of them living together as one they would perpetuate their species. From two of them, through a long line of ancestors, the Hidery have descended. At first the new made people had long arms and legs and were consequently unable to walk upright, were covered all over with hair, and had no clothes. From such a low starting point, by always selecting the fittest to survive, the finest looking as well as the freest from hair, for wives and husbands, the present race was evolved. After many lives (ages) had passed and the people had less hair to cover them, the climate began to get colder. Then the people had to cover themselves with skins, and to seek shelter in holes in rocks and in the ground, and finally to make themselves houses. It was then that the raven god, Ne-kilst-lass, tried to get them something to warm themselves by. I shall now give the Hidery version

OF HOW THEY FIRST GOT FIRE.

Ne-kilst-lass heard that a great chief who lived on an island in the Pacific had all the fire in the world. So donning his coat of feathers he flew over to this island. Reaching the chief's island he soon found his house. After a long conversation with him about the merits of his fire, Choo-e-ah seized a brand and with it flew over again to the mainland, letting fall, as he passed along, a few sparks amongst certain sorts of wood and stones. This sort of wood and these stones absorbed all the fire and gave it out again, when struck with a hard substance. The wood also gave it out when two pieces were quickly rubbed together. The Hidery say, when Choo-e-ah reached the land, part of his beak was burnt off.

YETHEL THE RAVEN GOD AND HIS SALMON WIFE.

This is a tale of Southern Alaska. Our aborigines, like more civilized nations, made their own gods. They first ascribe to them good or bad habits as suits their inclination. Thus they profess to follow the example set by them, whence the remark of the Thlingat of Southern Alaska, "As Yethel was so are we." Being very fond of games of chance, they say they are so because Yethel set them an example and quote the following story of Yethel, the stump, and his salmon wife. Yethel, they say was very fond of gambling; long ago he had a great game with a stump, which beat him so badly that he lost every thing he had. At that time he had a salmon for his wife. Now this wife had been very busy during the summer season drying salmon and packing them away for winter use, until she had a large number of boxes stowed away. When Yethel found the stump had got everything he had, he became so angry that he went home and beat his wife most unmercifully. This was too much for her, so out of revenge she restored all her kindred, the dry salmon in the boxes, who along with her ran into the river and away, leaving Yethel in poverty.

THE STORY OF YETHEL AND A FLOOD.

The Thlingat of Alaska, have the following story of a great flood. During the course of ages, existing conditions in course of development brought on a flood of water which covered the whole earth and destroyed all the people but a few who were saved by fleeing in their canoes to a very high mountain, where they lived until the waters left. Yethel saved himself by sticking his beak into a cloud and so held on until the waters left. When they left he fled down to earth and joined the remnant who were saved. They had left the mountain in search of their old homes. Arriving where they thought they once lived, they found all changed. Being few in number they were disheartened and felt badly the loss of their relatives. Yethel seeing their despondency told them to cheer up. He had come to help them, and if they would do as he told them they would soon have plenty of companions. "Gather," he said, "everyone, in front of you a pile of stones, then throw them over your heads backward and await the result." This they all gladly did, and as soon as these stones touched the ground they jumped up men and women. Thus they soon had plenty of companions and the world was repopulated.

I shall now give a raven story of another sort. It is from the Hidery and is a very old story. I have been creditably informed that the Japanese have long had a story of the same sort, and it is well known that more than once an island has been found in the South Pacific, on which there were only disconsolate women; all the men had been killed.

HOW THE RAVEN GOD HELPED THE WOMEN.

Long ago, on an island, far away on the big sea (Pacific) were a lot of women; all the men had been killed in war or taken away by some other means, of which there is no traditional record. The poor women missed the companionship of the other sex so much that they were utterly broken-hearted. In their lonely condition, an earnest, sincere and heart-felt desire for help went up to the raven god, who out of pity for them, picked up a young man and flew over to the island with him, and left him with the women.

The Alaskans have often told me while collecting Folk Tales amongst them, speaking of the raven god, "So much can be told about Yethel and his deeds that no man can tell them all." I, myself, am much in the same box. I know so much about Yethel that I feel I must give another story before I take up the eagle phratry. The one I am about to give is a tradition of the Queen Charlotte Island Hidery, and is as follows:

THE FEAST OF THE RAVEN GOD, NE-KILST-LASS.

Long ago, Ne-kilst-lass, wishing to give a great feast to all the people of earth, took a trusty bow, with quiver full of arrows, in order to provide a goodly supply of food for his future guests. After hunting over hill and dale, by lake, river and stream, he obtained a supply, which he set about to prepare for his guests. When all was ready, he invited his guests in a very peculiar manner, as follows: Turning to the east, he stamped his foot on the ground. No sooner had he done so, than a large number of people of a different language and color from those around, came in their canoes. These he welcomed to the feast. Then turning to the north, he again stamped his foot, with like results. This time a people different from all others in language and color arrived in their canoes; they also were welcomed to the feast. After their arrival he turned to the west and stamped on the ground, with the same results. Turning to the south, his stamp brought a fourth people in their canoes. These, also, were a different people, distinct in language and color. When all these various peoples or nationalities had arrived, the feast proceeded. After several days of feasting, dancing and singing, all the provisions being exhausted, and every one having received a present, this motley group left for their several homes.

The above story, it needs to be remarked, is not a totem tale. It is an ancient allegory of man's life on earth, and may be explained as follows: When the raven god Ne-kilst-lass had the feast ready, that is, this world fitted up and supplied with provisions of all sorts fit for food for the use of mankind, he invited to a feast, that is, to earth life, four races of mankind, of four different colors, of four different nations and languages; that is, red or brown, white, black and yellow. I have never yet been able to find which came from the east, or which from the north, or any other quarter ; but whether yellow, white or black, they came and had their share of the feast, that is, this life, and its good and evil, joys and sorrows. When the feast, this life, was over, all left for their own homes, that is, their life after leaving this world. So, as an allegory, this is very good. With it I finish the raven and take up the eagle.

THE STORY OF THE EAGLE.

Like the raven, the eagle is a phratry or brotherhood, and has fourteen representative crests, namely : eagle, raven, frog, beaver, shark, moon, duck, codfish, wasco, whale, owl, dog-fish, dragon-fly, and sometimes the sculpin. With some tribes the eagle is the highest; with others, the raven. Like the raven, the eagle is often placed on top of the mortuary columns, with the difference that the beak of the eagle is always turned to the right, with the exception when it is shown as slachan or phratry ; otherwise, its beak is straight. As a reason for its beak being twisted, the Hidery tell the following story : "One day the eagle was out walking with his first cousin, the raven, when the eagle said to him : 'How is it that you have given something good to all the inhabitants of earth, while to me, your cousin, you have given nothing?' 'I will give you something ; come here.' So the raven took hold of his beak and twisted it to the right, saying, 'I make you a slachan, and as such I have given you a mark to be known by.'" The Hidery also say the eagle is a fool and a simpleton, and as a proof of this assertion, quote the following : "One time the eagle had a nice lot of eatables in his house, while the raven had nothing good at all ; so, in order to get at the eagle's store, the raven sent him a long way off on a fool's errand. During his absence the raven turned to and ate up all he could find, leaving the poor eagle a bare cupboard."

I shall now give the story of the eagle as it is shown on the totem pole of the house of the eagles in the miniature village.

The name of the house is *coot-nass*, eagles' house. On the totem pole are two divisions; the husband's occupies the lower half, while the wife's is the upper half. The husband was a bear of the raven phratry, as is shown on the post. His wife was an eagle of the eagle phratry. The figures carved on the column connected with the story are, first (reading up): An object with a head somewhat like a seal. This is Ah-seak mentioned in the story. Above that are the eagles (including the king) mentioned in the story. The scene of the story is laid in the southern part of Queen Charlotte Island, British Columbia, and is in the Skiddance country, of which Captain Skiddance is chief, the country and village being named after its chief. The Hidery, when speaking of a great chief, always call him king instead of chief.

THE STORY.

Long ago a king lived in Skiddance's country, who had a sister and her family living along with him. Tradition does not give the number of her family, but only mentions one boy, the hero of this story. This boy was displeasing to his uncle, who made the child's life so miserable that he decided to leave the house forever. The uncle intercepted his plan by turning him out of doors. After wandering about a while, he was found by three women, one of them being ahead of the others. One of them, the first to find him, was the daughter of a king, the king of the eagles. Seeing him so sorrowful and woe-begone, she asked what ailed him. He told her all his troubles. Hearing them, she said, "Come with me to my father's house." She then took him into the timber. They had not gone far until they found a town, up on a tree. This was the eagles' town. A large number of eagles were flying about, who lived in this town. She took the boy home with her and made him comfortable. After awhile she presented him to her father, the king, saying, "Father, I have found a nice husband." The old man was highly pleased to see such a nice looking son-in-law. The boy, as I shall still call him, soon gained the old man's favor by doing many little things for him. If he wished for anything, off he went and got it for him, as the following will show. One day the old king said he would like to get a piece of whale's flesh. As soon as he said so, the boy dressed himself with a suit of the old king's feathers, and flew seaward until he found a number of whales. Off one he cut a piece and returned. This promptness pleased the old king greatly. After this the boy was so much pleased at being able to fly, that he was not contented unless he was always on the wing, and wished to have a suit of feathers for himself. So, in order to obtain his wish, he and his wife agreed to ask the old man. This they did. When he heard their request, he readily consented and without delay went to a box from which he took feathers enough to make the boy a full-fledged eagle. Some time afterwards, the old king, wishing to get some more whale meat, asked the boy if he would go and get it. Hearing this, the boy dressed himself in his new suit and left, returning in a short time with a whole whale. While off catching the fish, he saw so many everywhere that he spent the whole of his time flying about amongst them, leaving early and only returning after night-fall. Seeing his fondness for catching and flying about among the whales, the old king told him, if, while flying about he ever came across Ah-seak, above mentioned, he was not to take hold of it, nor even touch it, because it would do him no good. Some time after, while flying around and not thinking of Ah-seak, he saw a strange looking object floating about. In order to see what it was, he flew down and took hold of it. As he did so, it took hold of his hand and pulled him down under the water and held him so that he was unable to get up, one arm alone being held above water, and remained so. Next day, seeing he did not return, all the young eagles went to look for him. After flying about over hill and dale without finding him, they thought of Ah-seak. When they reached its place and saw the upheld hand, wondering what it could be, one after the other took hold of it, in order to pull it out. As fast as they did so, they, too, one by one, went under, until not one was left, the arm of the last one being held above the water, they all forming a line below. Seeing that neither the boy nor any of her family returned, the old mother eagle, the queen, suspecting something wrong, went to seek for them. When she came to the place where Ah-seak lived and saw the upheld arm, she knew at once what was wrong. In her case, Ah-seak had no power. She could take hold with all freedom of the upheld hand, and doing so, she pulled them all out as they went in, the boy last. At the same time, making a few passes over them with her hand, she restored them all. Having made them all well and strong, she said, "What are you all doing here? Go home and never be seen here again." This they all did, a wiser and a happier lot. Ah-seak seems to have been a sort of octopus, or devil-fish.

THE SUN TOTEM AND ITS STORY.

The sun, like the moon crest or totem, belongs to the raven phratry or brotherhood. Of the two crests, the sun ranks highest. It is generally painted as a face with points or rays around it. Amongst the Hidery tribes the sun and moon are painted much alike. The sun totem never had so many representatives in Hidery land as among the main-land tribes, from whom the Hidery seem to have adopted it with all its stories. When shown on the totem poles, in front of the Haida houses, it generally represents the sign of their raven god Choo-e-ah or Ne-kilst-lass, who got the box containing the sun from the old chief Settin-ki-jess, from whence he put it in the heavens. On the totem posts it shows that either the man who built the house or his wife and family belonged to, or were connected with, the sun crest. Not only was the sun a crest, but to a certain extent they used to offer prayer to it. A sample which I give is a prayer in wet weather: "Oh, thou good Sun, look down upon us. Shine on us, oh Sun. Take away the dark clouds that the rains may cease to fall, because we want to go a fishing (or hunting, as the case may be). Look kindly on us, oh Sun; grant us peace in our midst, as well as with our enemies. Again we ask, hear us, oh Sun!"

This is from the Simsheans, on the Skeena. I had it from Mr. George Cunningham, of Port Essington, on the above river. I have given it as near to the original as I can remember.

THE DAUGHTER OF THE SUN.

Far down in the dim and distant past, in this part of the world, lived two brothers, who both about the same time took to themselves wives. In due season these wives presented to each of their husbands a baby, to the one a boy and to the other a girl. The names of each I never could learn. As suiting the dis-

position of each, the boy I shall name Sun Cloud and the girl
I shall name Snow Flower. The boy, always plain, grew more
so as years passed over him, until he came to be considered the
plainest person in the village. Although endowed by nature
with little facial beauty, he was of a loving, kind and gentle disposition, ever ready to help the needy, or to say a kind word to
the down-hearted ; in fact, his was a noble soul within a rough
exterior. A dark and dreary storm cloud may hide the face of
the sun, yet withal, he shines behind it in all his wonted splen-
dor ; such his name, Sun Cloud, implies. The girl, always fair
of face, grew fairer every year, and when she reached her teens
was considered the prettiest maiden in the village. Soon she had
plenty of admirers and flatterers, who told her, a willing listener,
that she deserved the handsomest as well as the richest man in
the village for her husband, and if they were as pretty as
she was, they knew whom they would have. Many a good looking young fellow sought her company, in order to be able to
boast that he had walked or sailed with the prettiest girl in the
whole village. With all her beauty, she sadly lacked the better
qualities of her noble-minded cousin; she was cold-hearted, co-
quettish and proud. Those who knew her best said, "She was
as beautiful as a mountain flower and as cold as the snow bank
behind which it bloomed,"—whence her name, Snow Flower.
These two cousins, living near each other in the village, were
often in company. While out together fishing, she would steer
from place to place, while he watched the lines. Again in the
berry season, they would often spend days in each other's company, gathering a stock of wild fruits. In those days no thoughts
passed between them but those of friendship. By and by, a time
came when Sun Cloud, following the natural bent of mankind,
cast about him for a wife. For a long time he had a kindly feeling toward his fair but fickle cousin. Something he had, scarcely
could he tell what it was, that made him feel better while in her
company, and sad in her absence. At last a time came when he
revealed to her his feelings and asked her to become his wife.
She looked at him and replied she was too young yet to think of
marriage. Hearing her say so only served to make him press his
suit with more earnestness and candor. Finding that amongst

the number of her admirers she had one, at least, who was serious, in order to annoy the others, she very foolishly led him to understand that she loved him more than all the others, while, in fact, she did not care much for any of them. Her ambition led her to have lots of beaux, in order to make other girls jealous of her. With this assurance of her favor, Sun Cloud pressed her to name the day when he could claim her as his bride and so be happy, because without her he could never be anything but miserable. Thinking to tire him out of his love making for her, she tried the following game : Finding he was ever ready to do anything for her, or to go anywhere, however far it might be, to get her anything she wished, she would ask him to go to such and such a place for her, telling him each time he went that when he returned she would try and let him know when she would be ready to marry him according to promise. When he returned and reminded her of what was said before he left on her message, she only laughed and said she made it only to try him. Also, she would ask him to do many things, with the same promises. When done, every one had the same results. One day, returning from a long journey on her behalf, being tired and hungry and doubtless not in a cheerful mood when she told him she was not ready, "What do you mean?" he asked her. "I now see you are only fooling me; it is very unfair of you to serve me so. You ought to be ashamed of yourself to use me so." "One thing more," she said, "I shall ask you to do for me; if you do it, I shall then know that you truly and sincerely love me. This once, and I shall ask of you no more; so, when it is done, come and claim your reward. My request is this, cut your hair short. If you do not do it, let me see you no more. Go and think over it."

Here let me pause a while in the course of my story, in order to say a few words by way of explanation. Until recent times these people kept slaves, which they acquired by warfare and by purchase. In order to distinguish these from free men and women, their hair was cut short and kept so as a mark of subjection. A free man or woman by having the hair cut short, not only lost caste and became on a level with the slaves, but could not re-enter their own caste until again their hair was long. By making this request of him, no doubt Sun Flower firmly believed he would not on any account do such a thing, even if his expressions of love were true. Then if he failed to do so, she would consider herself clear of him. No doubt, when Sun Cloud heard this last request, he had a hard struggle within himself, a struggle between true love and dishonor.

Reaching home, true love prevailed. He went to a friend's house and had a close cut. Afterward hoping all would be well he went over to her house, in order to claim his reward. As soon as she saw what he had done for her love, she said, "You fool, do you think I would wed a slave? No, never. Go, and let me see you no more; when I wish to marry it will be with a free man and not with a slave." With these remarks, she turned and left him disdainfully. This was a death blow to his long cherished hopes. It was more than he could bear. So, sad and sorrowful he turned away and wandered onward he knew not whither, without resting or sleeping. Life at length became to him a burden, which led him to wish for a lonely place where, unknown and unseen, he could lay down and die. Wandering thus aimlessly about, he at length came to a house. Unwilling to be seen, he was passing quietly by when a kindly looking woman came out. Seeing him so sorrowful and so woe begone, she told him to come inside and rest awhile, which after a deal of pleading on her part, he consented to do and went inside. In answer to her question of what was the matter with him, he told her all, from first to last. When he had finished a recital of his troubles, she addressed him thus : "Before you came hither I knew all about you and your troubles; you have told me all and kept nothing back. Had you kept any of it you might have fared worse. As a reward for your many hardships, you before long shall get the best wife, as well as the prettiest in the land. Your wife shall be the daughter of the Sun. Before you leave this house, you must rest and have some food, after which I will show you the way to where she lives." When he was ready to depart, she went outside with him and showed him a narrow way leading straight onward from her house. "You must," she said, "follow this pathway, turning neither to right nor to left until you reach an exceedingly high mountain, up to the top of which you must climb regardless of every difficult place you may find in your way. Always look onward and upward, never look back. When you gain the top you will find the path still leading onward. Follow it until you reach a large and beautiful palace. If you do not see any one, knock and some one will come, who will inquire what you want. When they come, tell them that the old woman who lives beyond the mountain, sent you to marry the daughter of the Sun, and remember her only you must choose. These are my instructions; you know the way; farewell." With a light heart Sun Cloud pursued his course along the narrow path way until he reached the mountain. Looking upward along its steep and craggy side, his heart failed him. After resting awhile, he thought, if I try and get to the top I shall be well rewarded for all my misfortunes. If I lose heart and return I shall be worse of than ever before. I shall try, I will never look back until I gain the top. So thinking of nothing but onward and upward he finally, after a deal of climbing, reached the top.

Here we leave him to rest awhile and look ahead. From the top of the mountain, where he sits is another pathway leading to a large and beautiful mansion in the distance. This is the palace of the Sun, to which our hero is bent; on it his hopes are centered. In it he will find the fair one, he has come so far to meet, the daughter of the Sun.

Being rested and fresh he again started on his travels, happy in the thought of being so near the end of his journey. His expectation seemed to lend swiftness to his feet for in a little while he reached the palace. While seated on the mountain, he was dazzled by the distant refulgence of its buildings. Looking around, he saw no one, and everything being so beautiful, he was afraid to knock; after awhile he mustered courage and knocked. In answer to his call a man came, who asked him what he wanted. After delivering his message, the man opened the gate and made him welcome. After remaining a few days, during which he related to them all his misfortunes, telling them of the false promises of the girl he loved so well, how on her account he left home and friends, how he wandered aimlessly about until he arrived at the woman's house, where he was kindly cared for and directed on his way to this place, where he was to be provided with a better wife than if he had married his first

love.   After hearing his pitiable story, they said they could help
him in his search for a good wife.   So saying, they sent and
called the daughter of the Stars, a pretty little maiden with bright
twinkling eyes.   In answer to the question of how he would like
her for his wife, he replied, " She, no doubt, is as good as she is
pretty, yet, some how I feel she is not the one I came so far to
get." So they sent her back and called the daughter of the Moon,
who came and stood before him in all the splendour of her cold
radiant beauty.   Gazing at her for some time in silent admira-
tion, he at last said: "She seems so pretty and yet so cold that I
feel she is not for me."   So they sent her away and in her stead
brought the brightest and best of all, the daughter of the Sun.
When she came our hero was so dazzled with her beauty that he
was unable to look on her for a long while.   At length taking
her by the hand, he said :   "Thou daughter of the Sun! much
have I suffered and far have I come to meet thee.   Now that I
have found you I am like a new man.   In fact, I consider myself
well repaid for all my past sorrows and troubles, in as much as I
have found such a wife."   After awhile they together paid a visit
to his relatives at the home of his childhood.   All were glad to
see them and to welcome them home.   Soon every one in the
village was enchanted by the lady's loveliness and also by her kind-
liness of disposition.   To the sick her presence had a healing vir-
tue, which soon restored them to health and strength.   When
the sorrows of the heart sought relief by a flood of tears, her
kindly smile cheered the heart and dried the tears.   Loved and
respected by all the people, they lived happily together until a
ripe old age, while a long line of their descendants call themselves the children of the good daughter of the Sun.   As for Snow
Flower, when years with lengthening numbers passed along her
pathway, leaving her but little of her original beauty and having
nothing better to offer, no one seemed to care for her, which led
her sadly to regret the lost chances of bygone days.   Soon she
was glad to take for a husband one whom all the girls had refused.   She also became comparatively unknown, whereas her
cousin with better qualities and his estimable wife soon became
a power in the land.

THE MOON CREST AND ITS STORY.

.The moon as well as the sun crest belongs to the raven phratry or brotherhood. The moon crest is found in every village of the Hidery, as well as amongst other tribes in Alaska and British Columbia. In this paper I shall speak of the moon crest and its story. This story seems to have been taken from the ancient mythology of these people, showing at the same time the connection of the family, wholly or singly, with the moon crest. A house without a totem pole in front and in its place a painting of the moon in a very conspicuous part of the building, shows this house belongs to a person or a family belonging to the moon crest or totem. In the model village at the Chicago World's Fair, house No. 2, or the first painted house, was a miniature representation of the house in the village of Skidegat in which Captain Gold, chief of the moon crest, lived as late as 1894. On the front of this house, which is really the southern end of it, are painted the following: First, on top is a painting in a bluish color of a moon with a large hook nose. Under the moon, if I remember right, is a raven, also a man or two shown as if they were falling. The moon and all the figures represented on this house are parts of the following story:

THE MOON STORY.

The several parts of this story are rather disconnected owing to its being adopted by the Hidery, from whom I had it. I shall endeavor to give it in a readable form, keeping as near as possible to the original.

In by-gone ages a large town stood, either on the site of the present Port Simshean, an Indian town in Northern British Columbia, or somewhere near to it. This town at one time had a large population which, at the time of the opening of my story, was visited by a sickness so deadly that out of this large population only one solitary being, a woman, was left. The woman was sad and lonely, sad for the loss of her relatives and lonely because, in this plague-stricken town, she had no companions left. In order to see if there might not be a few still left she went from house to house with still the same results — dead, everywhere she went they were dead. With failing hopes she pursued her ghastly search until wearied nature demanded rest. She lay down and quickly dropped asleep. How long she slept she did not know. When she awoke it was bright day. As soon as she opened her eyes, she began to think seriously what would become of her, or what would she do. While engaged in this train of thought, a stranger, a man, suddenly appeared before her. At first she was surprised and somewhat afraid. At length she mustered courage enough to speak, saying: "I thought no one was here. Where did you come from?" "Above," replied the man. "I came from the moon; I have been sent here to bear you company." For a long while these two were the only people in town. As no one cared to come near, or to make their abode in town, they agreed to get married, then go to the man's home in the moon. This they did. Shortly after making their abode in the moon, the woman gave birth to a son, whose father was the man to whom she was married. Before going further I must say, by way of explanation, that the big nose and the blue on the moon, seem to denote rank in connection with the moon totem. After the birth of the child, the big nose said to its mother, "Let me have the boy awhile." As soon as the big nose got a hold of it, he took it by the head with one hand and by its feet with the other. Doing so, he pulled on it until he lengthened him out to be a big boy. Here we will leave him and take up another part of the story. Afterward nine men came along — they were strangers looking for a home. As soon as the moon's big nose knew they were strangers looking for a home, he made a little house for them, in which he shut them all and would not allow them to go outside. This sort of treatment gave them a deal of surmising as to what was to be the outcome of all this. If they asked the big nose to let them out, it replied, "Wait a little," or "Not yet." After they had been shut up a good long while, with no prospect of being liberated, the boy came to them and said: "You do not belong here; this is not your country. You are nothing but slaves and will be so while you remain here." When the men heard this they were very sorry, because, in their own country, they were all free men of good standing. They told the boy: "There are ten in our family, nine sons and one daughter; for each one of us our father built a house. We left our own country because we had to fight. We do not wish to fight again, but will do it sooner than lose our liberties, which we dearly prize.'' Hearing these sentiments, the blue of the moon said if one of the nine would get a spear, and pierce one or other through the body, he would give to the other eight their liberty. This they don't seem to have done, because I find afterward that the whole nine of them were gambling. Afterward the losing ones seem to have accused the others of foul play. Over this they quarreled and fought amongst themselves until they were all killed. Their sister, who had just arrived, was shocked to see all of her brothers lying dead, whom she had come so far to visit. The sister, having in her pocket a very potent sort of medicine, put some in her mouth, chewed it awhile, then spat it on each in turn, who jumped up alive and as good as ever they were. After awhile they all fought again; as often as any of them got killed the services of the sister and her medicine soon put all to rights. It appears that the rest of the people began to be afraid of the brothers, their sister and her life restorer. They seem to have done in all things just as they pleased. In order to get them out of the way, it would appear that the blue on the moon sent to a far country for help against the nine, because, the story goes on to say, a lot of men came from a far-off country in order to fight the original nine. This time they seem first to have got a hold of the sister and put her where she could be of no use to her brothers. The new comers then went and challenged the brothers, who accepted the offer. The new comers had the best of the fray, for all the brothers were killed. The sister, being in bondage, could not help them. So this ended the nine brothers, all being killed and their sister a slave, where she could not come to resuscitate them.

By looking at the house next the stream, the one without a totem post, all the figures representing this story will be seen. The name of that house is *kung-nass* or moon house. The people who had the moon for their crest had one sewed on their blankets, generally of a different color from the blanket. A chief of this crest had one carved on his dancing head-dress.

I shall next take up the bear totem and give the stories connected with it.

TALES FROM THE BEAR TOTEM.

The bear crest or totem belonged to the raven phratry. On most of the pictures taken in Alaska of the totem poles, the bear is shown on top, while in the miniature Haida village shown at the late Chicago World's Fair, the bear is shown as the lowest figure on the poles. How this came to be, the following will explain: In almost all of the villages where these poles were used, the wife, being to a considerable extent the head of her family, had the highest place on the totem pole, and when her crest was a bear, of course, it was placed on top, and when the husband's was a bear it would be placed on the bottom. Also, this crest belonged to Alaska and to the northern parts of Hidery land, but not to many villages in the southern parts, only to the village of Skidegat, where it was introduced at a later date by one of the chiefs taking as wife the daughter of one of the chiefs of Skiddance, who was by birth a member of the bear clan. Owing to this crest belonging to a large number of villages, it had in consequence a large number of stories. The one I shall give first is the story of the bear, his wife and the man. In the model village above mentioned is a house, which is placed near the end on the right. This house has an eagle on top of each corner post. On the ends of the six roof beams are as many bears. On the totem pole the figures are seven in number, namely: the first and lowest is a man; the second is a bear; the third is a young bear; the fourth figure is a woman. These four represent the crest of the man who built this house, who was a bear. The other figures represent his wife who was an eagle. Her story has already been given in the story of the eagles.

THE STORY.

Long ago, somewhere in Alaska, lived a man, whose name tradition has not preserved. He had two dogs; the name of one was San-es-wha, that of the other Coots-es-wha. One day this man went a hunting, with his dogs, his bow and arrows, also a spear whose shaft was two feathers in length. He had not gone far when his dogs began to sniff and run ahead, the man following. They soon came to a house. It was the house of the bears. The man went to the door, at which the bear came outside, his wife following. Seeing the man, the bear took hold of him by his legs and was rising up in order to hug him. Seeing the bear's intentions, the man quickly put his arms under the fore legs of the bear and threw him over his shoulder. By the effort of throwing him, the man lost his balance. In order to save himself he put out his hands and in doing so got hold of the wife on a certain part of her body, which rather pleased her. After a while she went into the house and began to scratch a hole in the floor. By doing so she showed that she wished the man to remain with her. Meanwhile the bear, disliking such rough treatment, "cleared out" for the woods, where he remained a number of years, having gone, he said, in order to get some food. The wife, seeing that her husband had gone, and the man having gained her affections, took possession of herself and house. After living with her a number of years and having two children by her, the man said to her one day he would like to return to his own country, in order to visit his relations whom he had not seen for many years. The wife replied, "You may go whenever you please, but by no means visit your first wife, because you might not return to us." This he promised not to do ; so he got ready and left. After spending a few weeks amongst his relatives, he one day met his first wife, with whom he held a long conversation. During the interview his old love returned ; so he promised to live with her again and leave her no more, which he did. When the bear learned that the man did not return from his visit, he came back to his home and wife. Seeing she had two children to the man, the bear grew jealous and feared the husband might return. In order to prevent him from doing so the bear determined to get him out of the way. In order to effect his purpose he made inquiry as to his whereabouts. He found that the man lived by the sea-side, and that he used to sail about in a canoe. One day the bear, who was lying in wait for him, got a hold of the man while coming ashore. A struggle ensued in which the man lost his life, either by being drowned, or killed by the bear.

HOW THE BEAR STOLE HIS WIFE FROM THE HIDERY.

Looking over my papers a few evenings ago, I found the following tale of the bear totem, bearing date of May, 1870, the time it was recorded. My informant was a very intelligent Haida, by the name of Ya-Quahn, whose memory was stored with legends like the following, which he used to repeat to me of an evening, seated by the camp-fire:

"You ask me to tell you something of by-gone days. I will tell you a tale, as I have heard it told around the lodge-fires by the old people, in our long winter evenings. Long ago, as our old people tell us, the bears were a race of beings less developed than our fathers were. They used to talk, walk upright, and use their paws like hands. When they wanted wives, they were accustomed to steal the daughters of our people. This is simply a story of people belonging to the bear gens taking for wives the daughters of mothers belonging to another gens. In all old tales I have never found the name of the hero of the tale, and when a name has been given, it appears to be one given by the story tellers, rather than the original name of the hero. In this tale no name has been preserved, so I have given names of people I have known, Queen Charlotte Island Hidery. Quiss-an-kweedass and Kind-a-wuss were a youth and maiden in my native village; she the daughter of one of our chiefs, he the son of one of the common people. Both being about the same age, and having been playmates from youth, their fondness for each other was such that it was frequently said of them, "If you want Kind-a-wuss, look for Quiss-an-kweedass." This youthful fondness in later years ripened into a love so strong that they seemed to live for each other. While thus they loved each other, they knew that by the social usages of the Haidas they could never live as husband and wife, both being of one phratry, the raven. While thus they continued to love each other, time passed by unnoticed. Life to them seemed a pleasing dream, from which they were rudely awakened by their respective parents reminding them that the time had come for each to choose a partner in life from among the youths and maidens of the Hidery, such as would be in unison with their social laws. Seeing that these admonitions passed unheeded, their parents resolved to separate them. In

order to effect their purpose the lovers were confined in the homes
of their parents, but with them, as with more civilized people,
' Love laughs at bolts and bars.' They contrived to meet outside of the village, and made their escape to the woods, resolved
to live on the meanest fare in the mountain forest, rather than
return to be separated. In a lonely glen by a mountain streamlet,
under a shady spruce, they built a rude hut, to which at nightfall
they always managed to return, no matter in what direction they
went in search of food. While wandering about they were careful
lest they should meet any of their relatives who might be in search
of them. Thus they lived until the lengthening nights and stormy
days reminded them of approaching winter,with its cutting winds
and snows. Then it was that Quiss-an-kweedass found it necessary
to revisit his home, and resolved to make the journey alone, Kind-
a-wuss preferring to remain, rather than face her angry relatives.
Having to stay alone in the solitude of the forest, she urged him
to promise before nightfall of the fourth day to return, a request
to which he readily assented. Early next morning he made ready
to go. While he was making preparations, Kind-a-wuss thought
she would accompany him part of the way, in order to shorten
the length of his absence. As they walked along together they
discussed the probability of his receiving a welcome, until she
thought it advisable to return to the hut, which she did, little
thinking what would happen to each before they should meet
again. Leaving Kind-a-wuss to find her way back to her mountain home, let us follow Quiss-an-kweedass on his way to his
father's house. Leaving her he loved so well, he felt ill at ease
for her safety. When he reached home his parents kindly welcomed him, and made inquiries as to Kind-a-wuss, and her whereabouts since they had departed; and he told them all. When
they heard how they lived, and that she had become his wife,
their wrath waxed hot. They told him he should never go back
for they would keep him until she also returned, as they
would make him a prisoner, which they did. How and where
they kept him, tradition, as far as I am aware, does not tell. When
he could not get away he felt ill at ease with regard to her he left
behind. He urged his people to let him go and save her life, for
she would never return alone. They listened to his appeal, yet

thought differently, and still detained him. Seeing this, he grew determined to effect his escape, which he did, after being confined a considerable time. As soon as he was at liberty he made all haste to reach his mountain home, hoping to meet Kind-a-wuss, yet fearing something might be wrong. When he arrived at the place where he parted from her, he found by the footprints on the soft earth that she had started to return. Drawing near the hut he listened, but heard no sound, and saw no traces of any one having been there lately. When he went inside he was surprised and horror-stricken to find she had not been in the place from the time of their departure. Where was she? Had she lost her way while returning? Hoping to find some clue to her whereabouts he searched the hut, looked up and down the stream, through the timber, up to the mountains, calling her by name as he went along—" Kind-a-wuss, Kind-a-wuss, where art thou? Kind-a-wuss, come to me; I am thine own Quiss-an-kweedass. Do you hear me, Kind-a-wuss?" To these appeals the mountain echoes answered, " Kind-a-wuss." After ineffectually searching the country for a number of days, sorrowful and angry, he turned his footsteps homeward, grieving for the dear one whom he had lost, and angry with his parents, whom he blamed for his misfortune. Reaching home, he called the attention of the villagers to his trouble, and claimed their assistance, to which appeal a large number responded, among whom were the two fathers, one anxious for his daughter's safety, the other disturbed because he had detained his son. Early on the morning of the third day after Quiss-an-kweedass arrived, this party, with himself at the head, set out for a final search, determined to find her dead or alive. After a search extending over ten days, during which time nothing was found except a place where traces of a struggle were visible, the party gave up the search and returned. As weeks gave place to month*, and months to years, Kind-a-wuss seemed to have been forgotten, her name was seldom mentioned, or only as the girl who was lost and never found. Yet there was one who never for a moment forgot her, her lover, who believed her still alive, and did all in his power to find her. Having been so often foiled, he thought he would visit a medicine man, or as he is named by the Hidery, Skaggy (Ska gildia, long-haired one), who was clairvoyant, in order to see whether by means of his gift this man could reveal anything. On this idea he acted. When he came to the Skaggy, Quiss-an-kweedass was asked if he had with him anything she had worn. On leaving the hut he had brought with him a part or piece of her clothing, which he gave the Skaggy, who upon taking it into his hand, thus began : " I see a young woman lying on the ground, she seems to be asleep. It is Kind-a-wuss. There is something among the bushes, coming towards her. It is a large bear. He takes hold of her; she tries to get away, but cannot. He takes her away with him. They go a long way off. I see a lake. They reach the lake, and stop at a large cedar tree. She lives in the tree with the bear. She has been there a long time. I see two children, boys. She had them by the bear. If you go to the lake and find the tree, you will discover them all there." This was cheerful news to Quiss-an-kweedass, who lost no time in getting together a second party. This party was led by the Skaggy, who by means of his gift, soon found the lake and also the tree. There they halted in order to consider what was best to be done in case of anything happening. It was agreed that Quiss-an-kweedas should call her by name before venturing up a sort of step-ladder which leaned against the tree. After calling her several times she at length looked out, and said, "Where do you come from? and who are you ?" "I am Quiss-an-kweedass," said he. "I have sought long years for you; now that I have found you I mean to take you home with me. Will you go?" "I cannot go with you yet, because my husband, the chief of the bears, is not at home; I cannot go till he returns." After a little familiar conversation she consented to come down among them. After they had her in their power they carried her off with them, making all haste homeward. When they reached their home, her parents were glad to have their lost child again, safe and sound, and Quiss-an-kweedass to recover his loved one. Although at home, and kindly welcomed, she felt ill at ease on account of her two sons, and wished to return for them. This her friends would not allow, but offered to go and bring them. To this she replied that their father would not allow them to go away; "but," said she, "there is a way by which you may get them." That is, the bear made for her a

song, which he used to sing ; if they would learn it and then go
to the tree and sing it, he, the bear chief, would give them all
they wished.   After learning the song, a party went to the tree
and began to sing it.   As soon as the bear heard the song he
came down, thinking Kind-a-wuss had returned.   When he saw
that she was not there, he felt bad, and at first refused to let the
children go, but afterward consented when they threatened to
take them by force.

I shall here leave the party on their way back with the
two boys, and give the story told by Kind-a-wuss, respect-
ing the manner in which she fell into the power of the bear.
After she turned back toward the hut she had not gone far
before she felt tired and sick at heart for her lover; in order
to rest awhile she lay down in a dry, shady place, where she fell
asleep.   While in this state the bear came along and found her.
When she found herself in the bear's clutches she tried hard to
get away, but found her efforts useless, as she was completely in
his power; so he took her an unwilling captive to his home,
which was by the lake.   As the entrance to his house was rather
high above the ground, he had a sort of step-ladder made,
whereby she could get easily up and down, and he also sent
some of his tribe to gather soft moss wherewith to make her a
bed.   When she thought of her lover and her relations she used
to wonder why no one came to seek for her, and when the bear
saw her down-hearted, he would tell her to cheer up, and do all
in his power to make her happy.   As time passed on into years,
and none of her relations nor her lover came near her, she began
to feel more at home with the bear, and by the time the search
party arrived, she had given up all hope of ever being found.
The bear did all he could to make her comfortable.   In order to
please her, he used to sit and sing, and for that purpose had com-
posed a song, which to this day is known among the children of
the Hidery by the name of the Song of the Bears.

I have heard this song sung many a time and would be glad
if I could write it down ; but, unfortunately, my ability to write
music is deficient.   I am sorry that it is so, because there is a
host of ancient songs and tunes among these people which I
would like to preserve, but cannot on that account.   With regard

to the words of the bear's song, I had long tried to get them
from these people, but was unable to succeed until 1888, when I
obtained the song from an old acquaintance. Whether he gave
them correctly or not I cannot say, but I shall give them as I got
them from him. They are as follows:

I have taken a fair maid from her friends as my wife.
I hope her relatives won't come and take her away from me.
I will be kind to her. I will give her berries from the hill and roots
    from the ground.
I will do all I can to please her. For her I made this song, and for
    her I sing it.

This is the song of the bears, and whoever can sing it
has their lasting friendship. On this account large numbers
learned it from Kind-a-wuss, who never again went to live with
the bear. Out of consideration for her, as well as the many
troubles of the lovers, they were allowed to live as husband and
wife and dwelt happily together for many years in their native
village. As for the two sons, whom I shall name Loo-goot and
Cun-what, as they grew up they showed different dispositions,
Loo-goot keeping by his mother's people, while the other, following the father, lived and died amid the bears. Loo-goot,
marrying a girl belonging to his parental crest, reared a family
from whom many of this people claim to be descendants. The
direct descendant of Loo-goot is a pretty girl, the offspring of a
Hidery mother and Kanaka father, who inherits all the family
belongings. A small brook, which flowed by their mountain
home, grows in its course to be a large stream, up which every
season large quantities of salmon run. That stream is claimed
by the family to this day and out of it they catch a supply of
food.

This then is the story of how the chief of the bear crest got a
wife, as was told to me by my informant, Yah Quahn, in 1873.
I have heard it told often by others since then, and at each time
of telling a great deal of the original was lost or forgotten, showing, I fear, that after a few more years, these fine old legends
would have been lost beyond recovery, had I not collected them
when I did. This pretty girl of 1873 was still alive in 1897 and
still good looking. Her two boys are now young men.

The signification of the names of the two principal parties

in this tale is as follows: Quiss-an-kweedass means one who plats or measures pieces of land. Kind-a-wuss means one whose father belongs to one tribe and her mother to another.

STORY OF THE BEAR AND EAGLE'S CLAW.

Inside of the house in Skidegat's Town, Queen Charlotte Islands, the one occupied in 1880 by the then Chief Skidegat, was a totem post. On it was carved the following: First, the lowest, was a brown bear. Then next an old woman with long lip ornament. Above all was an eagle and a bear. The lowest, the bear, was the crest of the chief's wife. The old woman, with lip piece was doubtless the wife herself, the size of the piece showing her rank. The eagle on top with the bear represents the following tale of the totem.

Long ago the bears, just as they are now, were very fond of salmon. They very much preferred live ones, but owing to their having no claws to hold them, were obliged to be content with their meals of dead ones. When they put their paws on living ones, in order to catch them, the fishes generally wriggled themselves clear, whereas if the bears had claws or something in their stead, they could have held them. How they came to be provided with claws the following legend will show. This legend was told to me by a very intelligent Haida named Amos Russ. While rendering it into English I shall keep as near to the simplicity of the original as possible.

Long ago a bear who had come a long way over the mountains, in order to add a few fresh salmon to his bill of fare, found when he reached the level country a stream, in which a number of beautiful ones were swimming around. Being early in the season no dead ones were lying on the bed of the stream and the others were still quite lively. Seeing a number of nice ones in a pool he waded in, hoping to catch a few and take them ashore for his dinner. He was not long in the pool until a nice big one came along. He soon had his paw on its back, from which it soon wriggled itself clear. Again and again he tried to hold them as they passed along but always with the same result. Tired and hungry, as well as disheartened, he raised his eyes heavenward and made this request: "O thou great and good Ne-kilst-lass; thou who listens to the supplications of all thy creatures, and helpest them in all their troubles. I come before thee a poor and hungry bear, have traveled a long and weary way and have long been trying in vain to catch one of these salmon, in order to break my long and weary fast. Having nothing wherewith to hold them they all got away. Oh thou great and good God, is there nothing which may be given me whereby I may hold them? Hear me, oh Ne-kilst-lass, and send relief." An eagle on a neighbouring tree, who had been listening to his cry for relief, flew down beside him, saying, "I have been listening to your prayer and have come to help you; hold up your paw." So saying he wrenched off one of his own talons and planted it on the bear's upheld fore-paw, saying: "That will hold the salmon for you." This claw not only quickly took root, but at the same time all the other paws were well provided with claws, and afterward every bear that came into the world was well provided with them, and consequently never after was without a plentiful supply of fresh salmon in their season.

The original totem pole from which this story was taken is to-day preserved in the British Columbia Provincial Museum at Victoria. Also a model of this house with this totem pole inside is shown in the miniature village in the Field Columbian Museum, Jackson Park, Chicago. This model house stands in the middle of the village. The totem pole can only be seen by looking down the smoke-hole or in by the door.

THE STORY OF THE BEAR AND FROG.

This story, although connected with the Chooitza-ton or bear crest, is the only one in existence, as far as I have been able to learn, connected with the Kimquestan-ton or frog crest. I have been told that this was a secret society, belonging exclusively to women. This society had their "coffin house of the frog ton," *Sathling-nah-kimquestan;* I have been inside of it. Having seen it, I will give a description of it. It was, when I saw it in the summer of 1883, strongly built of cedar planks, enclosing a space twenty feet square. Its roof was nearly flat and covered with cedar boards. Right in the center of the house stood a huge wooden frog. Forming a square around this frog and six feet from it on each side were piled, one above the other, fifty or sixty coffins, that is, boxes of all shapes and sizes.

In each one were the dried-up remains of a human being. This story is from the Queen Charlotte Island Hidery; I give it here from its connection with the bears. It is as follows:

Long ago there were lots of frogs on these islands. Now there are few, because they have all left. How they came to leave was as follows: Long ago, a frog was walking and jumping about amongst the wild flowers in the woods, making a meal of every little fly he found on his way. After awhile he came upon a bear's road. This road he followed for some time, until he met a large bear coming along. Seeing such a diminutive object coming along on his pathway, the bear stopped awhile, looking at it, saying, "You ugly little brute, what are you doing on my path?" The frog said not a word, but began to swell up a little. Seeing this the bear picked him up, smelled him, held him up, turned him round and round, then set him down, saying, "You dirty little brute, you are too ugly for me;" so the bear passed on his way. The frog, after such rough usage, was so terribly frightened, that he could do nothing for a long time. The frog, mustering courage enough to move, went direct home, telling every living thing he met what a terrible monster he had seen, how it took him up and put him to its mouth, as if it would devour him, then after nearly shaking him to pieces, smelled him and then set him down and walked away, after calling him an ugly little brute. "Now," said the frog, "what is to be done? We must get him out of the way or we will be all killed, every-one of us." So they called together a council of all the frogs to meet on a certain day. At the council, the first frog gave a description of the bear in such a manner that numbers of the frogs nearly died from fright. Before the council broke up, they decided as follows: That it was useless trying to kill or drive away such a terrible animal out of the country. The best thing for the frogs to do, was themselves to leave. To the above decision they all agreed and left the country, one and all of them. Nowadays frogs are neither seen nor heard on these islands.

THE STORY OF THE MOUNTAIN GOATS.

The mountain goat is a crest of the raven phratry. It is not shown on any of the totem posts at the model village. It is shown as a head with two horns on top of the mortuary column erected to the memory of Chief Skiddance of Skiddance. This column stands in front of one of the houses. The figures on it are as folllows: The lowest a bear, Skiddance's crest; the second, the head with horns, showing that he was connected with the society of the mountain goat; the third, on top is the moon; on each side of the column are two little figures of a man and woman. The bear signifies greatness, the goat nobility, the moon height. Altogether the inscription reads thus: "Erected to the memory of the great, the noble and the high Skiddance, Chief of Skiddance, by his daughter and son-in-law, the two little figures." This story of the mountain goat does not belong to the Hidery; it is a story of the same totem belonging to the Cowitchian tribes of Vancouver Island. The name in the language of these people is pe-kull-kun, *pe* white, *kull-kun*, wild animal.

THE STORY.

"There was a time long ago, our fathers tell us, when our people, the Whull-e-mooch, (dwellers on Whull, Puget Sound, State of Washington) lived a long way further south than we their children do now. Northward from the sea coast to the farthest mountains, the whole country as well as the sea was covered with snow and ice, so deep that the summer heat failed to melt it. The old folks tell us that their fathers did not like the land they lived in, but were at a loss where to go. Southward lived a people they feared, because they were stronger than our fathers were; northward the snow and ice as well as the great cold prevented their moving in that direction. While they were discussing what to do, Spaul, the raven god, suddenly came amongst them. After listening to their grievances he said, 'I shall soon settle that difficulty.' So saying, he turned all the snow and ice into pe-kull-kun, and sent them to make their abode in the fastness of the highest mountains, where there would be plenty of food for them, while their flesh would be food and their hair clothing for the Whull-e-mooch for ever. After the snow and ice had all gone, the climate became warmer and the land drier, which enabled the Whull-e-mooch to move northward to where we, their children, now live and our fathers lived before us."

This tradition is remarkable from the fact that at one time this Pacific slope was covered with snow and ice. This the ice grooves, which everywhere abound, from the bottom of the sea to the tops of the hills, plainly show. It is not at all apparent that the Indians would ever think to associate these ice grooves with a period of snow and ice. It is a tradition of the settlement of this country after the glacial period.

WASCO AND THE STORY.

Wasco, the subject of this story, is one of the crests belonging to the eagle phratry. As far as I can learn a tradition of an animal which lived in the water and on the land has long lingered amongst the Hidery. Never having seen one, its traditional appearance along with its name wasco, were preserved. While making an image of it they had to follow the traditional description of what was evidently an alligator. In bygone days when the Hidery began to adopt animals as family crests, some one doubtless had heard of wasco and adopted it as his ton (crest). The name, as far as I am aware, is only applied to amphibious animals like the above. When the Hidery make a painting of a wasco the tail is generally turned up along its back; when a carving, it generally has no tail. With regard to its name, wasco, the following is rather strange. I have a work by Louis Fiquier, "The World Before the Deluge," in which at page 255 is a picture representing an ideal landscape of the lower oolite period. In it is shown a little animal with its tail like wasco's, turned along its back, and a young one holding on to it, while the mother is climbing up the roots of a tree. The name given to this animal is *phascolo-therium*. One day a Hidery man had this book looking at the pictures. When he saw the animal going up the tree, he called my attention to it, saying, "Here is Wasco." Looking at the picture, I found its name *phascolo-therium*, a wild animal. With the Hidery wasco was considered a wild animal also.

THE STORY.

Long ago, three men lived at Quillcah, an ancient village which stood at the head of a bay three miles west from the present town of Illth-cah-getla or Skidegat's town. In front of this village was a low but steep bank, over which the villagers used

THE THUNDER-BIRD.

A PIPE WITH WASCO AND WHALES.

to throw the refuse of their food. In time this became quite a large heap, in which they used to bury their dead, of which a number of skeletons were found a few years ago while leveling a site for the refinery building of the Skidegat fish-oil works. I first saw this place in 1869; then an old and dense forest covered it to the water edge. I have made this departure because I will have to mention this ancient village in a few of my stories. Part of the inhabitants of this village were the three men above mentioned. What their names were I am unable to say, because the name of only one has been preserved, that of the hero of this story whose name was Coon-ahts (whale catcher, I believe.)

One day they together left this village and went over the hills to a lake, several miles away. After spending several hours at the lake they prepared to return. Doing so they were surprised to find that Coon-ahts was absent. After calling him by name and waiting awhile without finding him they gave up the search and went home. In this lake the above mentioned Wasco had his abode, from which following the outlet he often went to sea in order to catch whales. While out a fishing he would frequently return with a number of whales on his back. Sometimes he had one, at other times more. The most he appears to have got at one time was five. These he brought ashore in the following order: one in his large mouth, one between his long ears, two along his back with their tails on each side, and one under his tail. It certainly was a powerful sort of an animal to be able to do such feats.

There was, it seems, a belief amongst these people, that whosoever could kill Wasco and wear his skin, would become as strong and be as able to catch whales as he was, more so while clad in Wasco's skin. It is also told that he had a fondness for sharpening his appetite on young children, but this part of the tradition is not generally believed.

In order to try what could be done, one man had been scheming to catch him and that man was our hero, Coon-ahts. He had left the others, in order to make a trap wherewith to catch Wasco. This they did not know. A trap to hold such an animal must have been not only large but extra strong. Coon-ahts found from observation that Wasco, going and returning, always walked in the outlet. Consequently a strong beam placed across the stream, to which a number of ropes with a running noose were attached, could not fail to catch him in one or other of them. Looking along the stream for a suitable place he found a tree growing close to the river. Then he felled a stout tree across the river, close along side of the standing one, to which he bound it firmly with a strong rope. Then he crossed over the stream and felled two stout trees. These he bound together like an X. Then he raised the two upper ends, dropping the two lower ones into holes he had dug for them. After having them firmly placed, he raised the end of the cross-beam and dropped it into the shears. His next step was to get a number of strong ropes. These he formed into running loops, tying them strongly to the cross-beam, each hanging low enough for Wasco to run his head into one or other of them while passing underneath. Having everything secure, he went home. Returning in a day or two, he found Wasco dead, having strangled himself while passing beneath. Coon-ahts' next step was to get Wasco out of the water in order to skin him, which he did without delay. Having done so, he took the skin and fitted it on himself, in a manner that in every respect looked like the original Wasco. When fully dressed a feeling came over him, which then and ever after he was unable to resist, which urged him to go out to sea and try to catch whales. Ever after, when any of the people wished a little whale meat all that Coon-ahts had to do was to get into the skin and off to sea.

Looking over my papers I find that tradition mentions two sorts of traps, one I have already given. I shall now give the other. In this one, as in the other, Coon-ahts made a pair of strong shears, then he went back and felled a tree so as it would fall into the X, with its top projecting over the stream. Then he trimmed off the branches, and cut the top to a required length over the animal's trail. Then from the tree he hung a very strong noose, in such a position that Wasco could not help running his head into it. The ropes he used were made from cedar saplings. When all was ready Coon-ahts hid himself and awaited the outcome. After awhile Wasco came along and ran his head into the noose and soon strangled himself. Then Coon-ahts left his hiding place and skinned him. These are the two traditional stories.

In the village of Skidegat, on the east side of the road from the shore through the middle of the village, stood a house named *Sen-i-coot-quin-nie*, house of contentment or the contented peoples' house. In the minature village this model house is No. 19, and also stands in the middle of the village. On the totem pole are three figures — first, Wasco, whose head is shown and a whale as if on its back ; second figure is a scannah, and the third, is a female doctor or medicine woman in full dress. She forms a continuation of the above story, which is as follows:

Long ago a Skaggy woman lived at Kie, near Skidegat. At that time the people were very much in want of food. At this time she came amongst them in her full regalia, with her clecha-darran, or circle of puffins' beaks in each hand, as is shown by the carving. Knowing them to be in want, she promised to bring them within three days food enough to satisfy their wants. Day after day passed until the afternoon of the third, when a number of whales appeared. When they got in shore, where they could be seen, there were three of them. Seeing the whales, she harangued the people, saying this : "You see," she said, "what I can do; see here, according to promise I have brought you not one or two whales; just look and see for yourselves; there are three of them and enough for every purpose." When she had finished her oration, Coon-ahts, who it was had brought in the whales, threw off his skin, jumped up and said : "It was I, not you, who brought in these whales." Hearing this, the old woman was so ashamed at being made a liar before all the people that she drop-ed dead where she stood.

The pipe along with this story shows Wasco with his load of whales. The three men on top of the totem pole attached to this house in the miniature village, and the man on each corner post are the taden skeel of the family, adopted through their con-nection with the Skidegat family. The family crests were first, the wife's which was a scannah of the raven phratry, and that of the husband which was a wasco of the eagle phratry.

THE SCANNAH TOTEM AND ITS STORIES.

The scannah or finback whale is so named because a long fin which it has on its back is generally seen above water, while the fish is floating near the surface. This sort of whale used to be very plentiful in these northern waters, and by observation I think it is still numerous. By some writers its name is given as *delphinus orca*, and by others as *orca ater*. The Hidery name for it is scannah. Amongst the Hidery there are two sorts, scannah and auch-willo; the former has one dorsal fin while the latter is said to have seven, never less than five. According to the Hidery the auch-willo represents the highest rank, while the scannah represents the commonality. How the auch-willo came to be the highest, the Hidery tell the following story.

"Long ago the scannahs could not agree amongst themselves, so in order to preserve peace, they agreed to have a king over them. So they sent a deputation to the walrus, asking him to be their king. This he refused to be. Then they sent to the dolphin and several others with the same result. When they could not get a king they applied to the god Ne-kilst-lass for help. To their request he replied, 'you shall have neither one nor other of those. This I will do for you. I will take one of your number who shall be your king, and as a distinguishing mark he shall have seven dorsal fins and his name forever shall be auch-willo.'"

In the model village at the late World's Fair at Chicago is a house with an auch-willo totem pole. The pole stands to this day in the village of Skidegat, but the house has gone. One branch of the scannah gens had for a distinguishing mark a scannah with a hole in its dorsal fin. This is represented in the miniature village as well as often shown in pictures of the totem poles.

The origin of this hole in the dorsal fin is as follows: The scannah was always dreaded, not only by the Hidery, but by all the tribes in Northern British Columbia and Southern Alaska as well, because it was the general belief that these whales always tried to break the canoes and drown the Indians, who then became whales. It is told, that long ago two Hidery belonging to Chief Klue's village went out in a canoe in order to kill some of these whales, apparently as a daring adventure. They had not paddled far out to sea before the canoe was surrounded by a great number of these evil creatures which were about to break their canoe in pieces. One of the men, grasping his knife, said to the other that if he was drowned and became a scannah, he would still hold the knife and stab the others. The second man holding to a fragment of the canoe, floated near an island and swam ashore. The first was drowned, but this companion who had escaped soon heard strange and very loud noises beneath the water, like great guns being fired. Presently a vast number of fish floated up dead and with them a large scannah, which had a large wound in its side from which much blood flowed. The Skaggy or medicine man of the village said afterward that he knew, or saw, that the one so killed was the chief of the scaunahs and the one Indian who killed him had now become chief in his stead, and took for the crest of his clan this hole in the dorsal fin.

This clan, at one time was very numerous and consequently powerful; they had a village of their own on the west coast of Queen Charlotte Island; its name I think was Teaen. For some reason or other, their powerful neighbors on the southern end of these islands, the Ninstints, declared war on them. After a long struggle the scannahs were vanquished by the Ninstints, a large number of them being taken prisoners of war and sold as slaves. As soon as they were left alone, the remnant of the scannahs took all their belongings and left their ancient home forever and settled at the head of a bay far north from their much loved Teaen. Here they remained in peace a number of years. Again their relentless foes, the Ninstints, found them. Again they fled northward, led by a Skaggy of considerable ability. Having fled in a hurry, they had neglected to take a supply of food along with them and consequently were soon in a bad condition. At this stage of affairs they all begged of the Skaggy to take them to where they could get some food. To this he replied : "Just wait a little and you will soon get plenty." After a while they came to a low, rocky shore with a low, level country behind. "Now," said their leader, "here is a wild looking shore; we will go into the best place we can find ; I am sure the Ninstints won't trouble us here." So in they all went. They were not long on shore before they found this place afforded but little shelter and about as little food. Seeing the poor resources of their new settlement the Skaggy said : "You shall all have plenty of food before long." Toward evening, after they had got a temporary house put up, and all feeling much the pangs of an empty stomach, all again asked the Skagga for the promised supply of food. To this he replied : "Tomorrow all of you look toward yonder little island and you will see plenty of food coming toward you." Next morning while a dark object was seen in the distance, coming toward the shore, some one went to ask the Skaggy what it was, but he was nowhere to be found. After watching it, they found to their surprise, it was their Skaggy coming, riding on the back of a large whale. He had, unknown to the others, gone out towards the little island and caught a whale. As soon as he was on shore, he said : "Here is the food I told you of, so now help yourselves." This they gladly did. Being still afraid of the Ninstints and the place being bleak and cheerless, having neither a harbor nor shelter of any sort, they were ready at any time to move. This they did before their supply of food was exhausted. As before their course was still northward until they came to the village of Kioostia, of which Edensaw was Chief. Edensaw and his people, knowing well their many troubles, kindly welcomed them and gave them a large flat on the northwest point of Queen Charlotte Island, at the entrance to Perry Passage, between the mainland of V. C. and North Island. There under the protection of Edensaw and his powerful tribe they built their future home and gave it the name of Yakh. Having made themselves comfortable, they next tried to fortify themselves by digging a ditch or moat from sea to sea across the point. This they filled with water by turning a stream into it. Then for further protection they raised a palisading within the circuit of this moat. Edensaw the chief, who was my informant, told me they did not dig this moat, if not, they must have repaired one made by an older people. Although they had comfortable homes on a beautiful tract of land, hard luck seems to have followed them, because in 1883, when I was at their village, it was in ruins and not a living soul of this once powerful tribe was left. First, children ceased to be born into the tribe. Then the few left died.

Then one by one the old folks passed away until one old man alone of all the others was left in the village. Then kind folks in the next village took care of him until he was gathered to his fathers. There being no one left to take care of the houses they soon fell to pieces. Even the tombs are falling and exposing the mummified remains of the dead. Even their tall elaborately carved totem poles are yielding to the inevitable. Passing through their ruined village one day I came to a little house about six feet square; looking inside I saw two or three coffins. Standing up against one of them was the insignia of the chief of this clan. On inquiry afterward, I found that this was the tomb of the last chief. When he died there was none left to take his place. As it may be interesting to some to have a description of his insignia of office, I will give it here. First a wooden whale fourteen inches in length. On its back was its dorsal fin about the same length, with the usual round hole in it. On the other side was a staff three feet in length, let into the fish's belly. As for the Skaggy going out to the little island and catching a whale and bringing it ashore, I can only say that it was firmly believed in by all the people. I have seen the place where they lived and the little island. It appears to be about ten miles from the shore.

In conclusion I may say a few words about the Ninstints tribe, so named after their chief. They lived on an island shown on the chart as Anthony at the entrance to Houston Stewart Channel. To-day this tribe are few in numbers and their village is almost a ruin.

I shall take for my first story

KEEL-COONUC, OR WHALE'S SLAVE.

At one end of the division behind the model Hidery village in the Anthropological building of the Columbian Exposition at Chicago, were several other models of Indian houses from different parts of British Columbia. In this smaller collection were two Haida houses. These were placed apart from the others, because they were part of Ninstints town, a village on the southern end of Queen Charlotte Islands. The name of one of the houses was *nah-heeldans*, house of the earthquake, because, it seems, while this house was being built, there was an earthquake.

A man named Quill-ance built this house; his wife was named Gawh-nutt. The figures on the totem post are as follows: First, the lowest, is a sort of fish which it is said was once very abundant in the waters on the Alaskan coasts and near Fort Simpson in Northern B. C. The name of this fish was Keel-coonuc or whale's slave, because it seems to have always gone ahead of the whale, in order to lead them to good feeding grounds. As the principal story connected with this is one belonging to the Scannah totem, I shall give it here.

THE STORY.

Long ago, at the Indian town Kitt-kathla, in Northern British Columbia, lived a man who by birth was half Kitt-kathla and half Billa-billa, a neighboring tribe. He always lived at Kitt-kathla. This man's name was Keel-coonuc and he is said to have been a Scannah in disguise. Walking along shore one day, he espied four men in a canoe, coasting along. They were out hunting and fishing. As soon as Keel-coonuc saw them, he made for the canoe and took possession of it and the men. He then pulled them under the water where he kept them a whole year. During the absence of the men, their friends, who had been seeking for them everywhere unsuccessfully, came at length to the brother of Keel-coonuc and asked him if he ever saw four men who some time ago went a hunting and fishing in a canoe. He replied, he knew nothing of them, but would ask his brother if he did, and would do all he could to find them. The friends replied they would be glad if he could, because their families were starving. The house in which the two brothers lived had no sides, only a roof, and was full of Scannahs. Amongst them were the four men kept as prisoners. When his brother asked him if he had at any time seen four men hunting and fishing in a canoe, he replied: "Yes, I have them all here." So Keel-coonuc went and drove them all outside, saying, "Here are all your friends; take them with you and go home." So all left for home, at which in proper time, all arrived in safety, after their initiation into one of the societies belonging to the Scannah crest.

THE SCANNAH TOTEM AND STORIES.

This, the second story of the Scannahs, is the adventures of

Scannah-gan-nuncus, while trying to find the beautiful queen of the Cowgans. The name signifies the hero of the Scannah crest; Cow-gans means wood or field mice (wood nymphs).

The following story I found amongst the Hidery many years ago. What I then learned was merely a fragment of the tale as I know it to-day. After first hearing it, I spared neither time nor trouble in order to obtain the whole, if possible. Although, after a deal of research, I have been able to add a great deal more to the original, I fear there yet remains a great deal of it stored in the memories of the old folks. What I do know, I give in this paper, telling it as nearly like the original as possible.

This is a story of the long long ago told amongst our people, the Hidery, that at Quilh-cah, about three miles west from the village of Illth-cah-geetla, or Skidegat's town, lived a boy whose name was Scannah-gan-nuncus. The boy dwelt with his aged nanie (grandmother). He was the youngest of a family of eleven sons. Both of his parents were dead, also his ten brothers, of whom I shall say more by and by. Excepting himself and the old woman no other person lived at that place. All the other Indians in that quarter lived on Maud Island, three miles to the west. Our hero and his grandmother belonged to a crest different from the others. Close to the house in which they lived were three stone canoes. What is meant by these I do not know, unless they are canoes made entirely by hot stones and stone implements, as used to be the case in olden times. This boy, it seems, was so weak and sickly that he could neither stand upright nor walk. His weakest parts were from the knees down. One day he said, "Granny, put me into one of those canoes;" which she did. After sitting in the canoe a considerable length of time, he became quite strong and was able to walk like any other person. After becoming strong, he used to swim about in the bay. One day, instead of a swim, he concluded to have a sail, and with this idea got his grandmother's aid to put one of these canoes on the water. While this was being done, two of them broke, but with the third they were successful. After this, instead of swimming, he used to sail about on the waters of the bay, gradually venturing farther and farther from the shore. One day, making a further venture than usual, he sailed up the Hunnah, a mountain stream emptying its waters into Skidegat channel, four or five miles west from the place where he lived.

Tradition says that this river in those days was three times larger than it is nowadays. At present there is seldom water enough to float a canoe, unless at high water. It is also related that the waters of the sea stood higher on the land than is now the case. Of the rise of the land, evidence is everywhere to be seen ; old landmarks show thirty feet.

After pulling up stream, he became tired ; so, in order to rest, he pulled ashore and lay down. In those days at the place where he went ashore were large boulders in the bed of the stream, while on both sides of the river were many trees. While resting by the river, he heard a dreadful noise up stream, coming towards him. Looking to see what it was, he was surprised to behold all the stones in the river bed coming toward him. The movement of the stones frightened him so much that he jumped to his feet and ran into the timber. Here he found he had made a mistake, because all the trees were cracking and groaning ; all seemed to say to him, "Go back, go back at once to the river, and run as fast as you can." This he lost no time in doing. When again at the river, led by his curiosity, he went to see what was crushing the stones and breaking the trees. On reaching them, he found that a large body of ice was coming down, pushing everything before it. Seeing this, he got into his canoe and fled toward home. Some time after this adventure with the ice, Scannah-gan-nuncus took his trusty bow and quiver full of arrows and went out in order to shoot a few birds, as well as to try and find where the beautiful queen of the Cowgans dwelt. Walking along the shore, he saw at a distance what seemed to be a man, standing on shore at the edge of the bush, looking at him. Wondering who the stranger could be, he walked over to him and hailed him. Receiving no answer, he went up to him, and was surprised to find only a stump having a top like a man's head. Turning to leave, a voice which seemed to come from the head said, "Don't go away ; take me down ; take me down." Hearing these words, he took the stump in his arms, pulling it down at the same time. This was a man under enchantment. Taking him down broke the spell, and he instantly was himself

again. When thus restored, he told our hero that long ago he
had been taking liberties with the Cowgans, who, as a punish-
ment had cast upon him a spell. Under its influence he was to
remain as a stump until a young man, who lived with his grandmother would come and set him free, and he, our hero, was the
welcome one predicted.

The Cowgans, or wood nymphs, were said to be a number of
undeveloped spirits, who always appeared as beautiful young
women and who lived amongst the woods and mountains. At
the head of these was a queen, remarkable for her beauty, and
who lived in a magnificent palace is some unknown locality. To
discover the palace and to see the queen was a thing permitted
to none, except to those who could show some good, unselfish act
or kindness done. The young men used to go to the woods and
mountains in order to find her palace, from which a great many
never returned, and of this number were the ten brothers of our
hero. These Cowgans, it also appears, used to seek the company
of young men and lead them on until they took liberties with
them, and when tired of their services would turn them into
stumps.

The stump man asked our hero if he would like to see the
queen and her palace, to which he answered, "Yes." "Well,
then, go your way until you find a lame mouse trying to run
along a big log. Be kind to it and it will show you where to go
and what to do." After leaving the stump man our hero did not
go far before he saw a poor lame mouse trying to run along a log of
wood. He watched it for a while and saw that it would run
a little way and then fall off. Seeing this, our hero would
pick it up and set it a going again on the log; again it
would fall off. At last it stopped trying and said to our hero,
"You are a good man and a kind one; instead of killing me
when I fell off the log, you picked me up and put me on again.
Many would have run after me and tried to kill me. You are
Scannah-gan-nuncus and you would like to see the beautiful
queen of the Cowgans. Your ten brothers also wished to
see her, but they could not because they were bad men. They
ran after me and tried to kill me. No bad man can try to kill
me and live to see the queen. That was why they all disap-

peared so mysteriously. By trying to put me out of the way, they all got put out themselves. Now, come ; follow me, and I will show you the queen and her palace." The mouse led and our hero followed through long grass, bushes and timber, until they reached a beautiful country, where everything was ever fair and young. After traveling across this region for some distance, they came to the palace. Anything so beautiful Scannah-gan-nuncus never saw, nor ever could picture in his imagination. "Now," said the mouse, "let us go inside and I will intro-duce you to the queen of the Cowgans." This it did, telling her he was a good and kindly man, who, unlike his brothers, did not run after the mouse to kill it, when it fell off the log. When they found the queen, she was sitting spinning with a wheel. She was so pretty and so fair to look upon that our hero nearly forgot him-self. The queen made him welcome, left her spinning and came and sat beside him, telling him that as he was a good man he was always welcome to her palace and whenever he decided to visit her, he had only to come to the log and he would always find her servant, the mouse, who would show him the way.

How long he stayed with her I have, as yet, been unable to learn. Thus much I can say, that his grandmother asked him where he had been so long. He replied that while absent he had been where few or none had ever been before ; he had visited the queen of the Cowgans in her palace.

Before closing this paper, I find it necessary for the proper understanding of a few points mentioned therein, to say a few words drawn from my own observation and research, and also from the report of Professor G. M. Dawson of the Canadian Geo-logical Survey, who spent a part of the summer of 1898 amongst those islands. I wish particularly to draw the attention of think-ing men and women to our hero's encounter with the ice. Who was the author of this story, or when it was adopted by the Scannahs, I cannot say. Doubtless a tradition of ice coming down the Hunnah was current at the time when the Scannahs chose that fish as their crest. This event must have happened very early in the settlement of these islands, for tradition says at that time only two or three families lived on the southeast side of these islands, and that, excepting our hero and his grandmother, who lived at Quilh-cah, all the others dwelt in a small village on Maud Island, a mile and a half west from the others at Quilh-cah. The Hunnah is a stream flowing eastward and southward until it falls into the Skidegat Channel from the axial range of mountains of these islands. Prof. Dawson says that everywhere on these islands we find traces or evidences of the descent of glacier ice, from the axial range to the sea, and describes a number of valleys where the action of ice on their hillsides is plainly shown. He also showed from evidence given that the final retreat of the valley glaciers would seem to have been pretty rapid. A few years ago I took an Indian with me up this river valley, in order to see for myself the effects of glacial action. After observation, I agreed with Dr. Dawson, as well as with tradition, that the retreat of the glacier down this valley from the place of its birth at the head waters of the Hunnah must have been pretty rapid. The great glacial period either lingered longer on these islands, or else a smaller glaciation at a later day must have taken place.

It is said when our hero saw the queen she was sitting spinning with a wheel; she must have been making thread with a spindle and disc. The Hidery used the same means as the Indians in other parts of America. Making thread for the Chillcat blankets is done in the same way to-day.

THIRD STORY OF THE SCANNAHS—THE ADVENTURES OF NUCH-
NOO-SIMGAT, ETC.

This third story of the Scannah totem has long been told by the Hidery tribes, who borrowed it originally from the Simshean tribes on the mainland of British Columbia, in whose country the scene of the story is laid. It is called "The adventures of Nuch-noo-simgat in search of his lost wife." The meaning of the name is, "Hear you what I say?" The Hiderys pronounce it Nah-nah-simgat.

The tale is as follows: At the head of a bay near the present town of Mithla-kathla, in Northern British Columbia, in by-gone days, stood a small Indian town in which lived Nuch-noo-simgat, with his wife and several other families. One day a beautiful white sea otter came into their bay and swam about in front of the village. In order to get it for its beautiful white fur, all the people got their bows and arrows and tried to shoot it. Nuch-noo-simgat's wife, seeing what was going on, called to them to be careful how they shot, because they might spoil its beautiful white fur. "Shoot it," she said, "on the end of its tail, where its skin won't be spoiled." They did so, got it ashore and skinned it. When they spread out the skin they found a few blood stains on it. In order to wash them off, Nuch-noo-simgat's wife waded out into the sea and all the others went home. Hours passed silently away and no appearance of her return. Her husband went to look for her. He found the skin washed ashore, but of herself nothing was either heard or seen. After days of anxious and fruitless search, Nuch-noo-simgat thought he would visit a Skaggy (medicine man), who was clairvoyant. The Skaggy told him that the Scannahs had got hold of her and had taken her home with them and that she was then living with the king in his palace, as his wife. So in order to find her, he had to take two servants along with him, a martin and a swallow; the martin to go on before and smell, the swallow to fly about overhead and watch. Both had to keep a strict lookout as they went along, then come and report what each had found. The Skaggy said they were to go on until they found a canoe, in which they were to sail to where they would find two heads of kelp. From the two heads they would find a road leading onward to the house of the Scannah. With these instructions, Nuch-noo-simgat got the two servants and started, determined to find his wife, if it should take years. After a long travel to no purpose, they came to the sea where they found a canoe. Seeing it, Nuch-noo-simgat said, "Let us go and try if we can find the kelp, from which the road leads onward." After a long sail they found the two heads, where between them they tied the canoe and had a consultation. The martin said, "We can only do this; you try to find the road and I will take care of the canoe in your absence; as for the swallow, he can go back and tell our friends." To this they all agreed. The swallow went home and reported and as for the others, the martin took charge of the canoe, while Nuch-noo-simgat went down under the water in order to find the road leading to the palace of the king of the Scannahs. From the two heads of kelp he was able to trace the road straight ahead. This he followed until he saw something moving about like worms digging up roots.

When he drew nearer to them he noticed they were a lot of blind geese. While digging about they jostled each other in their blindness. This led to quarreling and from that to fighting. As he drew near, they stopped their fight and all together said, "Helloa! here comes Nuch-noo-simgat; we smell him." It was then he got his name. While he was looking at them fighting, he saw three strange men coming along. When they got where he was and entered into conversation with him, they said they were all slaves sent by their master to get some dry hemlock. During their conversation one of the slaves said, "Look! there is a dry tree. I will go over and see how it looks." On reaching the tree, he found it to be old, dry and hollow. Seeing this, he went inside and sat down. While there he seems to have fallen soundly asleep. After a while the other two followed and began to fell the tree. When it was nearly down, one man with a strong blow sent his axe through the tree right into the mouth of the sleeper inside, who awoke and came out. After felling it, they all began to cut it up; while doing so one of them broke his axe. Seeing the broken axe, all of them felt very bad, saying, "What shall we do? Our master will be very angry with us when he sees the broken axe." Seeing their grief, Nuch-noo-simgat said to them, "I am traveling about, trying to find my long lost wife; if you will all help me to find her, I will mend your broken axe." To this proposition they all readily agreed. So Nuch-noo-simgat passed his hand along the two pieces after placing them together; after a few passes their axe was returned as good and as strong as ever it was. When they saw it restored, they told him they knew where his wife was, and for his kindly act they would take him to her. They said they would take him to a place where there was a fire and a woman standing by it, warming herself. This woman was his lost wife, but as a long time had passed since she left, he would not know her. In order to help him, they said they would put a large kettle of water on the fire, then one of them would get an armful of wood and place it on the fire. While doing so, he would throw himself down and upset the kettle in the fire, which would put it out; then all he would have to do would be to jump over and get hold of the woman, who, as soon as she knew who he was, would go home

with him, very willing to leave her Scannah husband, because
she was his long lost wife. They told him to keep a good hold
of her, because the Scannahs might try to keep her. If he had
a good hold, they could not take her from him nor keep her any
longer.

   Another version of this tale is to the effect that the Scannah
who took her away gave her for wife to another, whose name was
Scannah-cah-wink-a-dass. What the name signifies, I have as
yet to ascertain. The first part, Scannah, shows his connection
with the totem or crest of that name. The geese, it appears, were
all women, who, by some evil genii were enchanted and turned
into geese. These our hero restored and the men finished their
wood-chopping. After this agreement, all four, that is, the three
men and our hero, Nuch-noo-simgat, started on the road to the
house of the Scannah. Of the geese women, nothing more is
said. After traveling a considerable distance, they came to where
a crane was mending a canoe. As soon as he mended it
in one part, he broke it at another, this being done for a blind,
as he was watchman for the Scannahs outside of their abode.
When the crane saw the strangers approaching, he gave the
alarm. After watching the crane at work, they noticed he used
a feather for drilling the holes. Seeing the amount of time wast-
ed, as well as the trouble he was taking in order to make a hole,
they gave him an iron drill and showed him how to use it. (All
the Indians on this northeast coast use drills to this day. The
drill is used between both hands; motion is given to it by passing the hands backwards and forwards.) When the crane saw how
much faster he could drill a hole with an iron drill than by the
old feather style, he was very much pleased. As soon as he
knew what they had come so far to obtain, he promised there and
then to help them all in his power, although he was in the service
of the Scannahs, whose house was close by. Hearing their watchman's alarm, the Scannahs came in force to his assistance, in-
quiring what had happened. "Oh," he said, "nothing; only
seeing these four men coming and not knowing but that they
might be foes, I gave the alarm. Since they came and I know
who they are, there is no danger whatever, because they are all
my friends." So, hearing this, all the Scannahs went inside, some-

what displeased. After all was quiet, the four men, led by the crane, went inside. The crane introduced them as his dear friends, whom he had not seen for a long time. Inside of the house was a large fire. Along side of it stood a woman, who, with a few others, was warming herself. In order to cook a meal, one of the party got a large kettle, which he filled with water and placed on the fire. A second man went for a few sticks, in order, he said. to make a good fire whereby to boil the water. Nuch-noo-simgat all the while stood looking at the woman, as well as all around the house, but said not a word. Soon the man returned with the wood, which he commenced to put on the fire. In doing so, he seemed to over-balance himself and fell, upsetting the water into the fire, making a great dust and smoke, through which little could be seen. Our hero, who was prepared for this, jumped over and grabbed the woman by her arms, holding her fast, saying, "I am your old husband; I have wandered far and wide in order to find you. Now that I have succeeded, you must return home with me; will you?" "I will," she replied. The Scannahs, be-ing completely taken by surprise, made no effort to retain her. After thanking the others for their services, and bidding them all keel-slie (good-bye), our hero and his long lost wife started for home. Returning by the way he came, after a while they reached the ascent ending at the two heads of kelp, up which they went. Here they found the canoe where it had been tied, old and rotten. On its bottom lay the bones of the koo hoo (martin) old and mouldy, having long been dead. In order to restore the faithful koo-hoo, our hero took from his pocket some herbs which he al-ways had along with him, in order to meet any emergency. These he chewed and squirted their juice over the old bones, and under its influence the same old martin jumped up as good as new. The canoe also was restored under the influence of the same potent herbs, and in it all three pulled for the shore. Once more on dry land, they soon found the trail for the old home, at which in due season they all arrived in safety. There Nuch-noo-simgat and his wife passed the remainder of their days in peace and comfort; as for Martin, no more has been preserved of him.

I shall next give a Cowitchian story of how they got fire.

HOW THE WHULL-E-MOOCH GOT FIRE—A LEGEND OF THE COW-
ITCHIANS.

Our fathers tell us that very long ago the Whull-e-Mooch
did not know the use of fire, nor had they any occasion to use it,
their flesh meats being eaten either raw or sun dried. They had
no use for fire to warm themselves because they lived in a warm
country. After awhile their climate grew colder, and they wished
for something to warm the houses they had to build for warmth
and shelter. Once upon a time a number of them were seated
around a deer which they had just found in one of their pit falls.
While thus seated a pretty little bird came and hovered around
above their heads, as if either watching them or looking for a
share in the meat. Seeing the bird flying about, some tried to
kill it, while others more kind, said, "Little birdie, what do you
want?" To this the birdie replied, "I know your wants, and
have come to you bringing the blessings of fire." "What
is fire," asked all of them? "Do you," said the bird, "see
that little flame on my tail?" "Yes," said all. "Well that,"
said the bird, "is fire. To-day all of you get together a small
bunch of chummuc (pitch wood) wherewith to get the fire. Tomorrow morning I will come here early and every one of you meet
me here, bringing your chummuc." Early next morning all
arrived at the chosen place, where the bird was awaiting their
coming. "Have you all got your chummuc?" said the bird.
"Yes," said all. "Well, then," said the bird, "I am ready, but
before I go let me tell you, my fire can only be obtained on certain
conditions, these conditions are perseverance and well doing.
You must strive for it in order that you may think more of it, and
none need to expect to get it who has not done some good deed.
Whosoever comes up with me and puts his or her chummuc on
my tail, will have the fire." "All ready," said the bird, "I go."
So off it flew. All the people, young and old, women and children, followed helter skelter, over rocks and fallen timber,
through swamp and stream, wood lands and plains. Some got
hurt, others peeled their shins, falling off the rocks and over the
timber. Numbers had more than they wished of mud and water.
Others were badly scratched and had their clothes torn amongst
the bushes. Numbers turned and went home, saying that anything

so full of danger was not worth trying for.   Others gave out
through sheer fatigue.   Still the bird kept on.   At length a man
came up to it, saying, "Pretty birdie, give me your fire, I have
kept up with you and never did anything bad."   "That may be,"
said the bird, "yet you cannot have my fire, because you are far
too selfish.   You care for nobody as long as you are right yourself."   So away flew the bird.   Another man came up, saying,
"Pretty birdie, give me your fire, I have always been good and
kind."   "No doubt," said the bird, "you have, yet you cannot
have my fire, because you stole your neighbor's wife."   Away
again flew the bird.   By this time few of the people remained, all
having fallen behind in the chase.   At length the bird came to
where a woman was nursing a poor sick old man.   It flew direct to
where they were and said to the woman, "Bring here your chummuc and get the fire."   "Oh, no," said the woman, "I cannot do
so, because I have done nothing for it.   What I am doing is only
my duty."   "Take the fire and welcome," said the bird; "it is
yours, you are always doing good, thinking it only but your duty.
Take the fire and give it to the others."   So she put her chummuc on the bird's tail and got the fire, from which all the others
were supplied, and have never since been without a supply.   This
is how, in the long long ago, the Whull-e-mooch first got fire.

THE BEAR AND PRINCESS, A HIDERY TALE.

This tale I shall give as it is told by the Hidery, who seem
to have got it from the Alaskans.   Many years ago a house stood
in the eastern half of the village of Skidegat, named *cathlings-
coon*.   There is a model of this house in the Field Columbian
Museum, Chicago.   The figures on the totem post in front of it
are as follows: First and lowest, a bear eating a boy who, as the
story goes, got lost in the woods and was found by a hungry bear,
who ate him up.   The second is a sea otter.   The third is the
raven.   The fourth figure is a scannah with its tail around a woman's
neck, the scannah being the wife's crest, the raven showing her
phratry ; her husband's crest, being as is shown at the bottom, a
bear.

Connected with this woman is a story; she was a princess,
the daughter of a great chief.   She wore copper rings around her

ankles. She and her father, upon a time, went to gather a certain sort of stones. They had not gone far before they lost their way. They went on until they came to a man standing on the road with a bear beside him. When they came up the bear said to them, this is a funny sort of a man, he has bones and hair, yet he is half stone. After looking at the man awhile the bear asked where they were going. "To gather stones," they said. "Can I go with you?" said the bear. "Yes," said both. So they three went on together, until they came to a lake with a deep hole in it. This hole was the home of an otter whom they shot with bows and arrows, but having no canoe they were unable to get it. In order to do so, the old man made a canoe, in which they both set out to look for it. Sailing about looking for it the daughter's hook got a hold of what she believed to be the lost otter. But instead it turned out to be a scannah, her line having dropped into the house of the scannahs, one of which came up and tried to take her down with it. After getting away from the scannah they did not care to stop any longer looking for the otter. So they two started for home, leaving the bear to go where he pleased. When they arrived at the stone man, they found, where he stood, nothing but hair and bones.

The model of this house is placed between the 20th and 26th in the Museum, I am not sure which. The name of the house was *Tau-scho-ass*, that is, copper (with T) at the door of the house. This was so named because at one time, long ago, while all the people living in the house were inside, a copper with a T on it, came flying into the house and told the people, all of them, to make one like it. This is how the Hidery at first got tau-scho, or copper-cross money, or as they are erroneously named, shields.

There is another story of the bear and princess, or, not unlikely, another version of the same story, which is as follows: Long ago, the daughter of a great chief took her basket and went to the woods and hills, in order to gather berries. After wandering about a long while without finding any, she met a bear. "Can you tell me," she said to the bear, "where I can find good berries?" "Yes," said the bear, pointing to a pile of berries, "there is plenty of them; pick them up." This she was

in no hurry to do, disliking their filthy appearance. Just then
three men came along. Seeing her with the basket, they asked
her if she was out picking berries. "Yes," she replied, "and I
wish you would show me where I can fill my basket with good
ones." "The bear," she said, "wants me to take these," (pointing down to the mess on the ground), "and I can't get away
from him." "Come along with us and we will not only show you
where you can get plenty of berries, but we will take you away
from the bear, as well." So they took her along with them to
where there were lots of fine large and ripe ones. Here they
left her and went along on their journey, wishing her good luck.
After picking alone, she came to an old man, who was also picking wild fruits. Being glad of each other's company, they
picked along together until their baskets were nearly full. Just
then she saw the bushes shaking a little way off, and to her surprise, out came the bear. Glad of the old man's company, she
told him her troubles with the bear. "Never mind," he replied,
"the bear cannot hurt you while I am here. Now that our baskets are full, we will go home, after filling our water boxes; we
will also take a few stones with us, beside the water." Having
everything ready, they together started homeward and had not
gone far before the bear was seen running after them. "Now,"
said the old man to the girl, "throw one of the stones backward
over your head and await the result." As soon as the stone
touched the ground, up sprang a high mountain between
them and the bear. This gave his bearship a high mountain to
climb up and over, while to them yet remained the level
country. By this means they got far ahead of the bear,
who did not again come near them for several days. When he
did, the old man said to the girl, "Throw some water behind you."
This she did and water flowed out of the ground, which soon
formed a large and deep lake over which the bear could not get,
and no more was seen of him. As for the old man and princess,
they got home without further annoyance.

I shall next give a few stories from the mortuary columns of
the Hidery.

MEELAS' TOMB.

Amongst all of the Northern Indian nations in British Columbia and Alaska it was customary for a person, man or woman, to have a memorial raised by their relations showing the social standing of the party in his or her own village, or their connection, if any, with a neighboring one. Often a person would have his or her tomb raised years before death. Often, if a person died and was buried away from home, a tomb was raised to his memory in his native village. Sometimes the tomb was made in the shape of the crest of the party; for example, if the crest of the party was a fin-back whale, then the tomb was a fin-back whale; if a whale, the head was placed in the ground with the tail upward. Often a hole was made to represent the throat of the fish. Then a hole was made, giving access to the inside, and a block of wood was fitted to close up the hole. When the party died this block was taken out and the body placed inside, then the block was replaced and firmly fastened, and, last of all, the body was left to decay. Seven or more models of tombs were shown at the late Fair, and doubtless are still to be seen in the Museum. The first model on the south end of the Model Village was one of these tombs in the shape of a fish. The last one on the north end is the subject of the following story:

Sometime in the early seventies there was raised in the grave-yard at Skidegat, a mortuary column to the memory of Meelas, a young Hidery, a native of Skidegat town. This tomb is twenty-five feet in height, and still stands—1897. The carving on it is as follows: First, a salmon, and close above it a boy's head. Further up, a fishing net is shown. Perched on top of this column is an eagle. This eagle shows his connection with the eagle crest and phratry. As this eagle has no bearing on my story, I shall say no more about it—only of the net, the boy and the salmon. This young man Meelas made the acquaintance of a young Indian, of his own age, who was a native of a village on a large river in British Columbia named Skeena. This Skeena Indian (I never knew his name) invited Meelas to live with him on the Skeena. This he did; and three years passed before he returned to his native Queen Charlotte Island. While living on the Skeena his friend, who belonged to the secret society of the Salmon, had Meelas initiated into his society. His initiation entitled Meelas to have a mortuary column with the above mentioned carvings, and the following story:

THE STORY.

Long ago an Indian family lived in a village on the banks of the Skeena. How many in the family there were, tradition has not preserved, one boy, the hero of our story, only being mentioned. One time his father made him a present of a nice copper collar to wear around his neck. After wearing it several years, he suddenly disappeared. In order to find him his parents, joined by all the neighbors, searched for him everywhere, without success. Finally tired and disheartened they all gave up the search, expecting never again to see him alive. Even his father, although unwilling to give up the search, finally had to follow suit. When any one spoke of him it was of the boy who went away and never returned. Although his parents had given over the search, they still fondly hoped to find him, believing him still to be alive. While cherishing these hopes, little did they deem that in a strange way he was yet to be restored to them. Winter, like other winters before, with their snows and rains, had come and gone. Summer once more had returned, bringing along with it leaves, and flowers, and salmon to the rivers. In order to have a change of diet, the old man one day took a fish net and placed it in the river. After awhile he hauled it in and found a good sized salmon. This he quickly took home to his wife. In order to prepare it for dinner, as is generally done, she commenced to cut off its head. To her surprise, she found while cutting around its neck, a copper collar. This discovery led to an investigation, which ended in the restoration of their long lost son, who by the enchantment of some evil genii had been turned into a salmon and placed in the river. In order to resuscitate him the old man went into the timber, where he gathered a few sprigs of a very potent herb. These he dried before the fire and rubbed into a powder between his hands. This he blew over the fish. It broke the spell and liberated the boy, who was thus restored to his parents as good as when new.

I shall next give the story of Skaggy Bealus, a remarkable story of the Hidery.

THE STORY OF BEALUS.

During the greater part of 1869 and the spring of 1870, I, along with fourteen others, had a long stay on Queen Charlotte Islands amongst the Hidery. We were employed building a tramway in order to ship coal. When we got under way, we found it necessary to add fifteen Indians to our number, in order to clear away the timber before the graders. These Indians built themselves houses along the north shore of the bay, at whose head stood the house in which we lived. In the third or fourth house of the row to the left of us, I noticed that an Indian ceremony was performed often nightly, if not, at short intervals. These ceremonies were generally kept up till midnight, often till near day-break, and almost every meeting ended with a weird, mournful song. What they were doing, and their song, I wished very much to know, but was unable to learn for some time. All I could get from them in answer to my question was, "We are talking to our dead relations." To me that was very unsatisfactory. At that time there was quite a number of boys and girls in our small village, and these young folks and I were fast friends because I used to give them rides on an ox-sleigh I had for hauling ties for the rails. From them I not only learned all I wished to know, but also got an invitation to their meetings, that I was to be sure and come on a given night because on that night a great doctor was to be there from the neighboring tribe of Gumshewa, whose name was Tow-a-tee. On the given night I went after supper, and some of the young folks who had been looking for my coming met me at the door and showed me to a seat. As soon as I had time to look about me I found the following: There were about twenty-five people of both sexes in the house. They were all squatted on the floor in a horse-shoe circle. Each had a stick in his or her hand with which they all beat time, on a board in front of them, to a song. Inside of the broad end of the circle a fire was kept burning. Within the narrow end of the circle sat Tow-a-tee. He would talk awhile and every one would listen. When he stopped, they all commenced to sing. I noticed that every time he spoke his voice was different. This seance, for such it was, they kept up till one o'clock, when they finished by singing the same weird

A SKAGGY OR MEDICINE MAN.

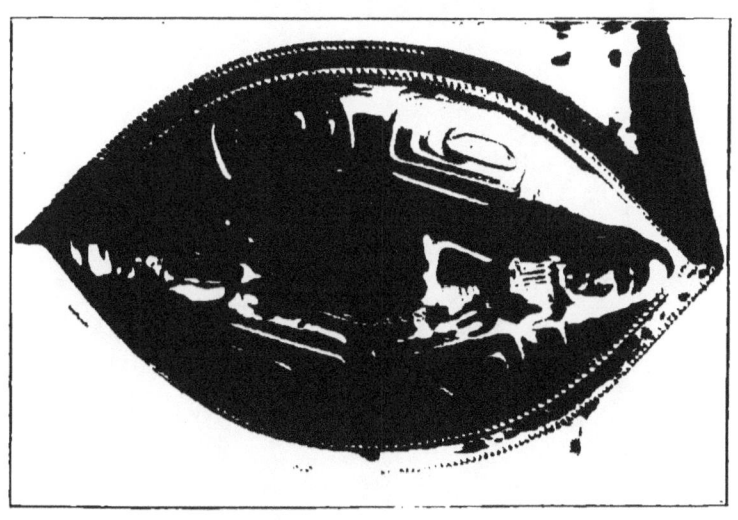

A DISH WITH CARVINGS OF TWO DOCTORS.

song.   Next day I made inquiry as to the signification of the whole affair, and was told the following: One year before a large number of these people had died of small-pox.   When any one dies the women blacken their faces and never clean them again for one year.   Toward the close of the year they have a seance, at which those who die of the small-pox, for whom they have mourned a year, control the medium, and give their several experiences since they entered spirit life.   In answer to the question, if they were happy and if they would like to return to earth life, each one replied they were perfectly happy and would not return to earth life if they could, and that it was needless to mourn for them any longer.   Such was the sum and substance of that night's seance.   Next day every one had clean faces.

With regard to the song, the Hidery say their fathers learned it ages ago from a great medicine man (Skaggy) whose name was Bealus.   He was a man of a fair complexion and had considerable of a beard.   He taught them a great many useful things and always told them to love and be kind to each other, and try and stop all intertribal wars.   If they did so, they would become great as a people, and others would respect them.   If not, they would become few in number, and at last a fair-skinned people from the rising sun would take possession of their country and finally their individuality would be lost in the others.   When these people came they were to be kind to them and trade with them, because they would give them a new sort of food and better implements than their old stone ones.   The Hidery say we settlers are the fair people and the new food is our flour or biscuits, while our axes and the iron adzes or tools traded by the people who visited them toward the close of the last century are the new implements.   After living amongst them many years Bealus told them he was soon to leave them and at the end of a year he would return and never again leave.   So one day he left suddenly.   No one knew where he went.   At the end of a year he reappeared as suddenly as he left.   After he returned, he lived to be so old, so says the tradition, that excepting his back-bone all the rest of his body was so shriveled that he could not use it, his back-bone only being fresh.   His whole life was spent in teaching them what was useful and good and to love and to be kind to each other. In fact, it is said that the last words he was heard to say were, "Love one another." He also told them that a sickness would come among them by which large numbers would die. He taught them a song or rather a lament for their dead relations and every time they had a communication with their relations in the better land they were to finish the sitting by singing it. I am heartily sorry that I am unable to give either the words or the music, for any thing so sad and mournful in the midnight hours I never heard. So much did it affect me that I could not keep from tears. The Skaggy Tow-a-tee came by request and each family who lost relations gave him for his service six blankets of the value of one hundred dollars, so after three days stay and a few more seances he packed up and left for home.

THE DOOM OF THE KATT-A-QUINS, A LEGEND OF ALASKA.

The following story I obtained during the summer of 1882, while collecting the Folk-Lore of the Southern Alaskan tribes. The Stickeen, from whom I had this story, live at the town of Wrangle, near the mouth of the Stickeen, a large river which rises in British Columbia, and after flowing through Alaska, falls into the sea as already mentioned. "Sticks" is the name given by the white settlers to the Indians of the interior and *heen* is the Thlingat for river or water; therefore, the term signifies the people living on the Sticks' river. Every summer these coast Indians go up the river to trade and at the same time lay in their winter stock of salmon; for, regularly every season, in order to deposit their spawn, these fish run up this river and its tributaries. Not only do they go to fish, but also to meet the Sticks, who bring down their furs in order to trade. Over one hundred miles up this river is a large flat, with considerable open land. On this flat stand a few houses, belonging to the chief of the coast tribe, who, like his fathers, on becoming chief took the name of Shakes. Consequently, the name of this small town was Shakes-heit, that is, Shakes' house. At this place most of the trading was done, although the coast tribes often visited the others in their own country. Several miles above this town was another large flat, on which the wild fruits used by these people grew in great abundance. To this flat, during the summer months, they used to come and get a supply of these fruits, which they dried and stored for winter consumption. Along the side of this flat the river runs in a straight line for a quarter of a mile, turning suddenly to the right on the upper end and in the same manner to the left at the lower end of the flat. In a line, across the flat and the river, stands a number of rocks, two large ones and three or four smaller ones. Excepting the two larger ones, which stand in the middle of the river, and one on the shore, all the others are on the level land beyond. The lesser ones are shaped like pillows, while the two larger ones vary a little and assume something of a triangular form. These rocks appear so strange that it is impossible for anyone to pass up or down the river by canoe or steamer, without wishing to stay and examine them closely. A geologist or a student of natural history would have little difficulty in solving the problem and explaining why the rocks stand as they do, like stepping-stones for some giant to cross. He would see that the rock, which on one side forms the river bank and bounds the plain, formerly extended across, making a lake above, with an outlet and waterfall over this ledge, which by some upheaval, probably, had blocked up the river, forming the above mentioned lake, in which had been deposited an immense amount of sediment brought down from up river. By and by, through advancing ages, the river in its downward flow, laden with ice in the spring and with timber and sediment in the summer, would wash away this barrier, leaving here and there a few patches of harder rock, which, finally, by the continued action of the water, became rounded into their present shape. As a natural consequence, the weakest part of this barrier would give way first, which would drain the lake and gradually form a new channel for the river, leaving the other portion dry, with its pillar-like rocks, whence the origin of this large strip of flat land and these strange rocks. If any person had been on this river, as I was in 1862, and had asked any of the Indians how these rocks came to be there, the answer would have been: "These stones are Katt-a-quin and his family." If asked who this person was, they would have given the following legend, long preserved among this people, together with many other tales :

Katt-a-quin was a chief among the Thlingat. He lived very

long ago, our fathers tell us, so long that no man can count the time by moons nor by snows, but by generations. He was a bad man, the worst that ever lived among our people. Not only were he himself and wife bad, but the whole family were like him. They were feared and shunned by every one, even by little children, who would run screaming away when any of the party came near. Nothing seemed to give them so much pleasure as the suffering of other people. Dogs they delighted to torture and tore their young ones to pieces. Most people love and fondle a nice fat little puppy, not so the Katt-a-quin family; when they got a nice puppy it was destroyed by hunger and ill usage. When the people met their neighbors from above, at Shakes-heit, if Katt-a-quin came there, he generally spoiled the market and if he could not get what he wanted by fair means he would take it by force. The people, seeing this, would pack up and leave. So tired had they grown of the family that the rest of the tribe had decided to make them all leave the village, or, failing in that, endeavor to get clear of them by some other means. But before doing anything of that sort, they were delivered in a way terrible and unthought of. From old versions of this story, it appears that the people had become so disgusted with the family that when they wished to go hunting, or to gather wild fruits, they would strictly conceal their object and the direction of their journey from those whom they disliked. One morning, while all were staying at Shakes-heit, they made up their minds to go to the large flat, where these rocks now stand, and gather a stock of wild fruits for winter use. So, in order that none of the Katt-a-quins might come, they all left early and quietly. When the others got up, which was far from early, as they were a lazy lot, and found that they were left alone, they were displeased at not being asked to go along with the others. After a time they all got into a canoe and went up the river in order to find the rest, which, after a while, they did by finding their canoes hauled up on shore. After this they also landed and began to pluck berries, but, finding that the people who preceded them had secured the best of the fruit, they gave up picking in disgust and were seated on the shore when the others returned, having, as might be expected, plenty of fine fruit. Seeing that the others had a fine supply, and they, themselves, nothing but sour, unripe stuff, they asked for a few, which the others gave them, at the same time saying they should not be so lazy, as they also might have got their share of good ones. After awhile, the old fellow demanded some more of their best fruit. This, the people flatly refused, saying the late comers ought to go picking for themselves. Just then, a number of the first party, who had gone in another direction, returned with baskets full of nice large and ripe fruit. Seeing this, the whole family of the Katt-a-quins went and demanded all. This, the others refused, saying they had no idea of toiling all day, gathering fruit for such a worthless lazy set as they were. A scuffle began, which ended in the family upsetting all the fruit and trampling it under foot in the sand, thus destroying the proceeds of a long and hard day's work. Seeing all this, the people made a rush, some for their bows and arrows, others arming themselves with whatever came to hand, all determined to wreak vengeance on those who had caused the destruction of the proceeds of their day's labor, and whom all disliked. Seeing this turn of affairs and the determination of the people, the offenders knew that their only safety lay in getting aboard their canoes and going down the river before the others could follow them. This they did, leaving in their hurry two or three of their children behind. As soon as they reached the middle of the river, a new and terrible retribution befell them. Yethel, the raven god, who had been watching their conduct, in an instant turned them all into these stones and placed them where they now stand, to be an eternal warning to evil doers. The largest stone is Katt-a-quin; the next is his wife, and the smaller ones on the land and in the water are their children. What is seen is only their bodies, turned to stone; their souls, which can never die, were sent to See-wuck-cow, there to remain for ages, or, until such time as they shall make reparation for the evil done by them while in the body. Afterwards, they will all ascend to Kee-wuck-cow, a better land. Such was the doom of the Katt-a-quin. "As our fathers told us the story," said the Thlingat, "so have I told it to you."

REMARKS ON THE ABOVE.

According to the ideas of the ancient Southern Alaskans, when a person died a natural death or was killed for his misdeeds, his soul was sent to a cold, desolate country, or a condition called See-wuck-cow, there to remain until he was sorry for his bad deeds and wished to make reparation for them. Then he would go to a better land above, called Kee-wuck-cow, life above. Those who fell in battle, fighting for their homes and country, always went to Kee-wuck-cow.

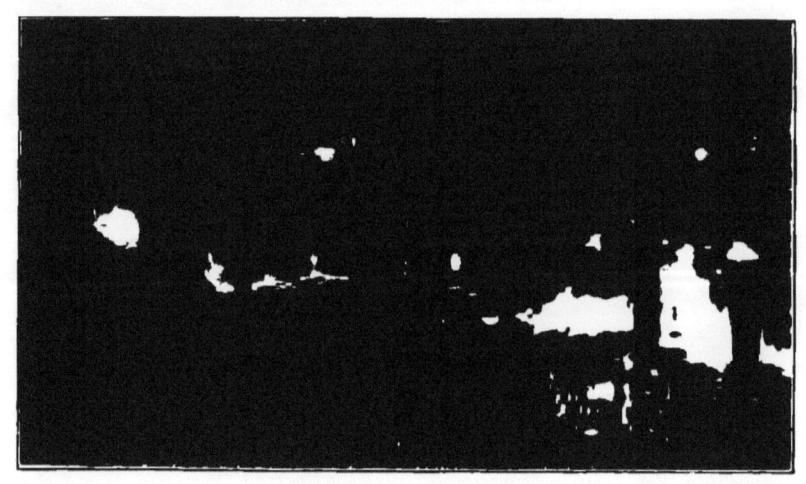

HOUSES AND TOTEM POSTS.

TOTEM POSTS AT THE WORLD'S FAIR.

(Reprinted from the AMERICAN ANTIQUARIAN, Vol. XV., p. 281.)

According to promise, I send you a short description of the carved columns or totem posts in front of the Haida house at the end of the south pond in the Columbian Exposition grounds. Properly considered there are only four Haida columns in Jackson Park, for the other four, although used very much for the same purpose as the columns, are of a different style and were used by a widely different people. While giving a description of the carved ones, I shall begin at the one on the north of the house, and go south. For the information of your readers, a correct reading of not only this totem pole, but of the others also, I will send you as near as I am able a definite interpretation of each figure. The inscription alongside of this column reads thus : *Totem pole or heraldic column of the Tsiw Indians.* The figures represent, counting from below upward, as follows : first, the raven; second, dogfish; third, man; fourth, wolf; fifth, the killer whale, and, sixth, eagle. On the above mentioned column, reading from below, the first is the carving of an Indian with his head encircled by feathers. This represents the party to whom belonged the house in front of which this column stood. The second figure is the raven, called by these people Cauch. This, the raven, is the phratry or principal crest, along with the eagle phratry of all these people. The next is the dogfish, which along with the raven phraty, was the crest of the man who had this house built for himself. The third figure is a man, perhaps designed to represent the man whose portrait this was, and to show that he belonged to the tribe amongst whom the house was built. By saying this I take a Haida standpoint; with the Simshians it may be different, although I hardly think so. The next or fourth figure above is a wolf. This is the crest of the wolf gens or crest. How it came to be placed there I can hardly say. This much I know: it showed a connection with that crest, or, in other words, a connection between the party who built this house and the clan bearing the wolf crest. The fifth figure is a woman with head-dress, and is evidently a figure of the housewife. Above her is the figure of a killer or fin-back whale, with two young ones, one on each side of its mouth. The sixth figure is the crest of the wife. The young ones show her to have had a family, which, like herself, would have the whale crest. The next or seventh figure is that of a woman, showing that the wife was connected by birth with the tribe in which she lived. The upper or last figure is the eagle, and designates the phratry to which she belonged. This column was part of a house which stood in an Indian town on Naas River, British Columbia. It was sent by a Mrs. Morrison, an exceedingly intelligent half caste, her mother being a native Simshian.

The second column, the one at the middle of the Haida house, is, of course, different, as it is a Haida column. This house formerly stood in the middle of the Haida Indian village of Skidegat's Town, so called from its chief always taking the title of Skidegat. His house belongs to a man whose name formerly was Chooeah, or raven. After the death of an uncle, his mother's brother, he inherited the uncle's property, and consequently took the uncle's name, which was Clads-ah-Coon. This house was first house in village belonging to the Cathlans-coon-hadry (point of the waves people), who came and settled in the town of Illth-cah-getla (hut between streams) called Skidegat's Town, as above mentioned. These people were driven from their home by tidal waves and by ravages of war. When they came to Skidegat they lived all together by building their houses in a row; their descendants live all together in same style to-day. The figures on the post are: lowest, the bear with man's head downward; second is the spout-fish (lown); on each side of it is the chemouse of the Simshians, which is a symbolization of a river snag, a floating snag or often a tree. To an Indian sailing down the rapid streams of the Pacific slope these snags are dangerous, and a superstitious dread has painted them as monsters

of the worst kind; so, in order to be safe, they adopted them as
a crest. The Haida tribes borrowed this crest from these Simshians. The next figure is a head with large eyes. It is shown
as holding on with its mouth to the tail of the lown. This is the
head of a bear as is shown by the *tan gue* (bear's ears) placed on
each side of the head. From this head upward is a large dogfish. It is shown as having a woman on its back. Above the
woman's head is another bear's head, with *tan gue*. Above all
is the tail of the dog-fish, shown between two little images. The
following I consider to be a correct reading of the carvings on
this post : First, the bear with a man's head downward; amongst
the natives of southern Alaska this symbolized a strange custom.
When any one built a house a slave was killed and his blood
sprinkled on the post, his body generally being buried beneath
it, the bear on the post being the crest of the man who built the
house and the man being the slave who was killed. I have been
unable to find that such a thing as killing a slave for such a
purpose was ever done amongst the Haida. In this case I speak
knowingly, as I helped to dig up the post, and I found that no
slave had ever been buried there. In fact the man who built the
house says he killed no slave.

There are two stories told by these Haida people with regard
to a man's head being upside down on the post. The first I shall
give is the one told by the builder of the house :· The bear was
the crest of the man Chaouk, by whom the house was built. His
intention being not to follow the old usage of his people by
having the doorway in the post, he had the man's head put on in
order to have no blank space, as well as to exemplify an old
story, which runs thus : Long ago, a little boy wandered away
and got lost in the bush. A hungry bear found him and ate him
up. The second story is founded on a usage common among
these people : If a man owed just debts to another, he was
politely asked three times to pay it, and if then he refused, no
more was said of the debt by the party to whom the money was
owing, but he quietly waited until he had money enough to build
a house, when, among other carvings, he had the image of the
debtor put on in the shape of a man with his head down, and his
crest above him, in order that the people might know who it

was. A debtor seldom waited until the third time, well knowing the consequences.

The next figure is the lown or spout fish. It was put on to show the crest of Choouto's first wife, who was a daughter of Crosaw, chief of Hieller, on these islands. The chemouse on each side was put on for ornament more than anything else, although no doubt there was a connection between it and the wife. The two bears' heads above show a double relationship between this chief and the bears, which came about as follows: He inherited his uncle's crest, which was a bear, as well as the bear crest of the village Cathlans-coon (Point of the Waves), in which he was born. Together with these heads is a woman's head and a dogfish. This represents an old legend among these people, the legend of Hathlingzo (Bright Sunshine). She was a woman who, long ago, went to the open country in order to dig roots for food. After she had plenty, she went to the seaside to wash them. While there a dogfish came along and turned her into a sort of mermaid—half woman and half dogfish. This is said to symbolize the storm clouds, which, in that land of mountains, often quickly turn the bright sunshine to a storm. This story may also symbolize the Cathlans-coon-hadry or people, when they left their own country and settled at Skidegat. The dogfish being the crest of the town of Illth-cah-getla, or, as it is generally called nowadays, Skidegat's Town, from the chief, who also takes the name of Skidegat, so by becoming that town's people, they became entitled to the dogfish crest. The two wooden men with the tail of the fish between them, with taden skeel on top, may signify this man and his uncle Clads-ah-Coon, and it may not. Probably they meant that he was a chief at two times or places. The three circles, black and white, are three degrees of aristocracy. They also show that he was allowed to have three dances, and to wear circles around his neck while dancing. This carved column is forty-two feet in length and is, like all the others, made of red cedar.

The third post is an Alaskan one from Tongass, on the southern boundary of that country. This one is also about forty-two feet in height. The carvings on it are: 1. The lowest, a bear holding a raven, although it looks more like a fur seal, which I should certainly say it was if the post was a Haida one. 2. Next above is a bear, a frog with a bear's tongue in its mouth, and a hat with eight rings. As for the signification of the carvings on this post, I may say that the bear at the bottom was the crest of the people whose house this was. The bear holding the crow or raven, as is shown here, would show that the bear and the raven were foes and that the bear had the best of him, though according to the Haida tribes it would show an old legend about the bear and the fur seals. 3. Next above was the phratry of the man who owned this house. He also was one of the Cauhada gens. 4. Next above is the frog with the bear's tongue in its mouth, which showed the bear and the frog to have been friends. This frog I believe is the bear's wife's crest. The highest figure —the head and hat with eight degrees—must have been the husband, because the hat is on a bear's head. This post is badly finished. A Haida carver would never put such a post out of his hands, and if he did he would be laughed at by the rest of the people.

The next column, fourth in order, is a Haida post. It is of far better finish, and is worthy of a Haida. This post has for its figures, first and lowest, a scamsum or sparrow-hawk, the doorway to the house being in the belly of the bird. The next is a frog; the next a being with a bear's head and a human body, holding on to the dragon fly; the next a crane; on the top is the taden skeel of three men, showing the chief's successors. This one, as well as No. 3, is exhibited by Mr. E. D. Ayer, of Chicago, Ill., to whom, I believe, it belongs. The description given of this post is rather imperfect, and a stranger could glean but little information from it. The large bird on the bottom can hardly be called the sparrow-hawk. It should be called the mosquito-hawk. The Haida legend of its origin is as follows: Long ago the land was mostly covered with water, and when the water left it was very swampy. Then the sun was very hot, far hotter than it is nowadays. This swampy ground bred mosquitoes of an enormous size; they were as large as bats. These bats are well known to most people from their habit of flying about by night. These insects were so large, and their bite so deadly that many people died from them. The country was slowly being depopulated from this cause. The people complained until the god Ne-kilst-lass heard their cry, and sent the butterfly to investigate. On its return, it gave a woful account of the people's condition. Hearing this, Ne-kilst-lass sent the mosquito-hawk to live on them and drive them away, which it did. Now that the sun is less hot, and scamsums plentiful, the people can live. One legend is that the scamsum was an enormous bird, which still lives in the mountains, from which it flies over the sea, in order to destroy the killer-whales, or, as the Haida call them, the scannah. Its body is the thunderbird, the clapping of its wings the noise, the lightning a fiery dart sent out of its mouth in order to kill these whales. The next figure is evidently a frog, showing that the party who had this house was allied to that crest or gens, or, what is not unlikely, they might have been connected with Skidegat's family. The next is rather difficult to decipher, owing to the head, which is evidently a bear's, being upside down. It has the *tan gue* (bear's ears) on it plain enough, showing it was highly connected with the bears. From its mouth to the mouth of the figure above is a band, which is held by the under figure. This shows a connection between the two. In the third post it shows friendship existed between the two figures— that is, the bear and the frog. In this case the animals shown are different. The lower figure I consider to be a bear, and the upper I believe to be either a butterfly or a mosquito, and doubtless symbolizes the old story of the butterfly sent out by the ancient god Ne-kilst-lass. The figure above seems to be intended for the dragon fly, which also is an enemy to these pests; although I consider this portion of the carvings to be neither more nor less than a rendering of the above legend. A number of years ago I saw in the old village Yukh, Queen Charlotte Islands, a rendering on a very old totem post of the same myth. The figure with the long beak is a crane, or heron, and doubtless was the crest of the wife of the man who built this house. The three figures on top belong to the family of Skidegat. The first chief of that name adopted it in order to have it on top of his column. It is a mythological tale of the west coast, and is as follows : Long ago the god Ne-kilst-lass, for a frolic, turned himself into a beautiful woman, and three men fell in love with her and, some say, married her, although this totem post shows it belonged to one of Skidegat's family. This ends the totem posts from northern British Columbia.

The next is a house of a different sort and belonged to the Quackuhls of Vancouver Island. Instead of a totem post these people generally paint their crests on the front of their houses. The paintings on this one represent the sun on each side of the doorway, with the thunder-bird above the door. This is the style of this bird, as is shown by these people. This house, the notice on side of the wall says, belonged to the Nu-enshu clan of the Quackuhls, on Vancouver Island, British Columbia. The next carving is a doorway from a house at Billa Coola, in the interior of British Columbia. It is a bear, and was the crest of the people who lived in the house. The next carving also was the doorway of a house, at Billa Billa. The paintings are as follows: Upper part, the raven; next, the spirit of the sea. This forms the doorway. The last two figures were part of a house of the Nannimoach tribe on Vancouver Island. They stood inside of the house and supported the roof beam. One of these post figures is represented as holding a goose in its hand. One or both of them represent the *Or*, a spirit of the sea, called by these people *swie-o-quie*.

OFFICERS.

OF THE

International Folk-Lore Association

FOR 1898-9.

President: Dr. Nathaniel I. Rubinkam.

Vice Presidents: Professor Frederick Starr; Louis J. Block;
E. W. Blatchford; Countess Evelyn Martinengo Cesaresco, Italy;
Hon. John Abercromby, England; David Mac Ritchie, Scotland;
Rev. H. F. Feilberg, Denmark; Henry Wissendorff, de Wissa-
kuok, Russia; J. B. Vervliet, Belgium; Arthur Gorovei, Rou-
mania; Professor Kaarle Krohn, Finland; Cav. Vid Vuletic
Vucasovic, Dalmatia; Michel de Zmigrodzki, Poland; Homer
B. Hulbert, Corea; Ernest W. Clement, Japan; Dr. N. B.
Emerson, Hawaii; Rev. Wyatt Gill, New South Wales; Dr.
Teofilo Rodrigues, Venezuela; Paul Groussac, Argentine Re-
public; Dr. E. Hoffman-Krayer, Switzerland; Dr. Cenek Zibrt,
Bohemia; Henry Gaidoz, France.

Secretary: Helen Wheeler Bassett.

Treasurer: Frederick T. West.

Directors: Mrs. H. W. Bassett, Dr. Oscar L. Triggs, Miss
A. E. Isham.

Curator: Dr. Selim H. Peabody.